'Andahazi deftly mines that delicious vein of wit and sensuality that runs from Boccaccio to Fellini, while slyly dissecting one of man's oldest obsessions: a woman's pleasure'
Laura Esquivel, author of *Like Water for Chocolate*

'*The Anatomist* must be read. Its themes, far from being scandalous, are ingeniously post-modern'
Noticias

'*The Anatomist* is a wonderfully comic excursus round the foibles of the so-called Age of Discovery. The novel dips from fable to farce and back again, with an adeptness which is as startling as it is compelling. Along the way, it skims other genres – courtroom drama, scientific treatise, even some Renaissance feminist poetry - with the same light touch . . . Beneath its glorious surface gloss as a beautifully structured critique of Rennaissance science and ignorance, the novel is also a history of the language of female desire and male attempts to understand and control it. Beautifully written and skilfully translated, this is a cunning, witty and brave book on the most fundamental of human desires which is not, after all, for sex but for control'
Ranti Williams, *TLS*

'Ever wonder who first discovered the clitoris? Probably not. Well, apparently it was a 16th-century Italian doctor and this quirky novel is loosely based around his discovery. Set in Venice, it tells the sorrowful tale of the imprisoned doctor's unrequited love and addresses the hypocritical morals that woman of the day were subjected to. Witty and audacious'
Kate Figes, *Elle*

REALDI COLVMBI
CREMONENSIS,
In almo Gymnasio Romano
Anatomici celeberrimi,
DE RE ANATOMICA
LIBRI XV.

The Anatomist

Federico Andahazi, in his mid-thirties, is an Argentine psychotherapist of Hungarian descent. He lives in Buenos Aires. *The Anatomist* is his first novel; his second novel, *The Merciful Women*, is now available from Doubleday.

Alberto Manguel is a well-known translator and critic. He is the author of *A History of Reading*.

Also by Federico Andahazi

THE MERCIFUL WOMEN

THE ANATOMIST

Federico Andahazi

Translated from the Spanish by

Alberto Manguel

BLACK SWAN

THE ANATOMIST
A BLACK SWAN BOOK : 0 552 99946 6

Originally published in Great Britain by Doubleday,
a division of Transworld Publishers

PRINTING HISTORY
Doubleday edition published 1998
Anchor edition published 1999
Black Swan edition published 2000

1 3 5 7 9 10 8 6 4 2

Typeset in 11/14pt Ehrhardt by
Phoenix Typesetting, Ilkley, West Yorkshire

Black Swan Books are published by Transworld Publishers,
61-63 Uxbridge Road, London W5 5SA
a division of The Random House Group Ltd,
in Australia by Random House Australia (Pty) Ltd,
20 Alfred Street, Milsons Point, Sydney, NSW 2061, Australia,
in New Zealand by Random House New Zealand Ltd,
18 Poland Road, Glenfield, Auckland 10, New Zealand
and in South Africa by Random House (Pty) Ltd,
Endulini, 5a Jubilee Road, Parktown 2193, South Africa.

Printed and bound in Great Britain by
Mackays of Chatham plc, Chatham, Kent.

CONTENTS

PART THREE
The Hearing

PART FOUR

PART FIVE

PART SIX

FOREWORD

THE DAWN OF OBSERVATION

'MY AMERICA, MY NEW-FOUND-LAND!' Mateo Renaldo Colombo (or Columbus, to give him his English name) might have written in his *De re anatomica*.[1] Not a boastful cry like 'Eureka!' but rather a mournful lament, a bitter parody of his own misadventures and misfortunes, compared to his Genoese namesake, Christopher. The same surname and, perhaps, the same destiny. But they share no common blood and the death of one takes place barely ten years after the birth of the other. Mateo's America is less distant and infinitely smaller than Christopher's; in fact, it's not much larger than the head of a nail. And yet, it was to remain secreted away until the year of the death of its discoverer and, in spite of its insignificant size, its discovery was equally momentous and disturbing.

It is the Age of the Renaissance. The verb is 'To Discover'. It is the twilight of pure *a priori* speculation and the abuse of

---

[1] *De re anatomica*, Venice, 1559, Bk XI, Ch. XVI.

syllogisms, and the dawn of empiricism, of knowledge based on what can be seen. It is, quite precisely, the dawn of observation. Perhaps Francis Bacon in England and Campanella in the Kingdom of Naples chanced upon the fact that while scholastics were lost in syllogistic labyrinths, the illiterate Rodrigo de Triana was, at the same time, shouting 'Land!' and, without knowing it, heralding in a new philosophy based on observation. Scholasticism (as the Church had finally understood) was not profitable enough or, at least, seemed less useful than the sale of indulgences, ever since God had decided to soak money out of sinners.

The new science is good as long as it helps to bring in gold. It is good as long as it doesn't contradict the truth of Holy Writ or, what is even more important, a magistrate's writ of property. Just as the sun no longer spun its path around the Earth (something which obviously didn't stop happening from one moment to the next), geometry had begun to chafe against the confines of its own paper landscape and had set off to colonize the three-dimensional space of topology. This is the greatest achievement of Renaissance painting: if Nature is written in mathematical characters (as Galileo says), painting must be the source of a new vision of Nature. The Vatican frescoes are a mathematical epic: witness the conceptual abyss that separates Lorenzo de Monaco's *Nativity* from *The Triumph of the Cross* over the apse of the Capella della Pietà. For similar reasons, not a single map is left unchanged. The cartography of Heaven changes as well as that of Earth and that of the body. Here now are the anatomical maps that have become the new navigational charts of surgery. And thus we return to our Mateo Colombo.

Encouraged perhaps by the fact of sharing a name with the Genoese admiral, Mateo Colombo decided that his destiny, too, was to discover. And so he set off to sea. Of course, his waters were not those of his namesake. He was the greatest anatomical explorer of his time; among his more modest discoveries is nothing less than the circulation of the blood, anticipating by half a century the Englishman Harvey's demonstration in *De motus cordes et sanguinis*. And yet, even this astonishing discovery is of little importance compared to his America.

The fact is that Mateo Colombo was never able to see his discovery in print, since his book was not allowed to appear until the very year of his death, in 1559. One had to be careful with the Doctors of the Church. The cautionary examples are almost too numerous. Three years earlier, Lucio Vanini 'chose' to be burned by the Inquisition in spite of (or because of) his statement declaring that he would not give his opinion on the immortality of the soul until he became 'old, rich and German'.[2] And certainly Mateo Colombo's discovery was far more dangerous than Lucio Vanini's opinion – even without considering the aversion our anatomist felt toward fire and the stench of burnt flesh, above all if the flesh was his own.

[2] A. Weber, *A History of European Philosophy*.

THE CENTURY OF WOMEN

HE SIXTEENTH CENTURY WAS THE CENTURY of women. The seed sowed a hundred years earlier by Christine de Pisan flowered throughout Europe with the sweet scent of *The Sayinge of True Lovers*. It is certainly not by chance that Mateo Colombo's discovery took place when and where it did. Until the sixteenth century, history had been recounted in a deep masculine voice. 'Wherever one looks, there she is, always present: from the sixteenth to the eighteenth century, always on the domestic, economic, intellectual, and public stage, on the battlefront and in moments of private leisure, we find the Woman. Usually, she is busy at her daily tasks. But she is also present in the events that build, transform or tear apart society. From one end to the other of the social spectrum, she occupies all places and those who watch her constantly speak of her presence, often with fear,' write Natalie Zemon and Arlette Farge in their *History of Women*.[3]

[3] *A History of Women in the West*, Harvard, 1993.

Mateo Colombo's discovery happens precisely when women, whose place had always been indoors, began to conquer, gradually and subtly, the world outside, emerging from behind the walls of convents and retreats, from whore-houses or from the warm but no less monastic sweetness of home. Timidly, woman dares argue with man. With some exaggeration, it has been said that the 'battle of the sexes' begins in the sixteenth century. Whether this is true or not, this is the age in which womanly matters become an acceptable subject for discussion among men.

Under these circumstances, what was Mateo Colombo's 'America'? No doubt, the borders between discovery and invention are far more vague than they might seem at first glance. Mateo Colombo (the time has come to say it) discovered that which every man has dreamt of at some moment or other: the magic key that unlocks women's hearts, the secret that governs the mysterious driving force of female love; that which, from the beginnings of History, wizards and witches, shamans and alchemists, have sought by means of brews, all manner of herbs or through the favor of gods or demons; that which every man in love has always longed for, when wounded, through unkindness, by the object of his troubles and sorrows. And also, of course, that which is dreamt of by kings and rulers in their sheer lust for omnipotence: namely, the instrument that subjugates the volatile female will. Mateo Colombo searched, traveled and finally found the 'sweet land' he longed for: 'the organ that governs the love of women'. The *Amor Veneris* (such is the name the anatomist gave it, 'if I may be allowed to give a name to the things by me discov-ered') was the true source of power over the slippery, shadowy

free will of women. Certainly, such a finding had many
serious consequences. 'To what calamities would Christianity
not be subjected if the female object of sin were to fall into
the hands of the hosts of Satan?' the scandalized Doctors of the
Church asked. 'What would become of the profitable business
of prostitution if any poor hunchback might obtain the love of
the most expensive of courtesans?' asked the rich proprietors
of the splendid Venetian brothels. And, worst of all, what
would happen if the daughters of Eve were to discover that,
between their legs, they carried the keys to both Heaven and
Hell?

The discovery of Mateo Colombo's America was, all things
considered, an epic counterpointed by an elegy. Mateo
Colombo was as fierce and heartless as Christopher. Like
Christopher (to use an appropriate metaphor) he was a brutal
colonizer who claimed for himself all rights to the discovered
land, the female body.

Beyond what *Amor Veneris* meant to society, another contro-
versy was sparked by what it was really supposed to be. Did
the organ discovered by Mateo Colombo actually exist?
Perhaps this is a useless question which must be replaced by
another: did the *Amor Veneris* ever exist? Ultimately, things are
nothing but the words that name them. *Amor Veneris, vel
Dulcedo Apeletur* (the full name with which its discoverer chris-
tened the organ) had a strong heretical ring to it. The question
of whether the *Amor Veneris* coincides with the less apostate
and more neutral *kleitoris* ('tickling'), which alludes to effects
rather than causes, is one that would later concern historians
of the body. The *Amor Veneris* existed for reasons other than

anatomical; it existed not only because it *inaugurated* a New Woman but also because it sparked a tragedy.

What follows is the story of a discovery.

What follows is the chronicle of a tragedy.

PART ONE

THE TRINITY

I

O N THE OTHER SIDE OF MONTE VELDO, IN the Via Bocciari, close to the Church of the Holy Trinity, stood the Bordello del Fauno Rosso, the most expensive whorehouse in Venice, whose splendor had no rival in the whole of the western world. The brothel's main attraction was Mona Sofia, the most expensive whore in Venice: in the whole of Europe none could be called more splendid. She was greater even than the legendary Lenna Grifa and, just like Lenna Grifa, Mona Sofia toured the streets of Venice reclining on a covered litter, borne by two Moorish slaves. Just like Lenna Grifa, Mona Sofia kept at the litter's head a Dalmatian bitch, and a parrot perched on her shoulder. In the *Catalogo di tutte le puttane del bordello con il lor prezzo*,[4] her name appeared printed in bold letters and her price in even more remarkable numbers: 10 ducats. That is to say, six ducats more expensive

---

[4] *Catalogue of all the Whores of the Brothel with Their Prices*: A catalogue mentioned in D. Merejkovski, *Leonardo da Vinci*, Putnam, 1992.

than the legendary Lenna Grifa.[5] In the catalog, carefully compiled and edited for discerning travelers, no mention was made of her eyes green as emeralds, nor of her nipples hard as almonds whose diameter and texture might be compared to the petals of a flower – if ever there were such petals of the diameter and texture of Mona Sofia's nipples. Nor did it make mention of her firm animal thighs, as if rounded on a lathe, nor of her voice like crackling wood. It made no mention of her tiny hands that seemed hardly large enough to encircle a male organ, nor of her diminutive mouth whose cavity one would have thought unable to receive a fully engorged member. Nor did it mention her whorish talents, capable of arousing even an enfeebled old man.

Early one winter's morning in the year 1558, shortly before the sun appeared halfway between the two granite columns brought back from Syria and Constantinople, crowned with the winged lion and with St Theodore, just when the auto-mated Moors in the clock tower were about to strike the first of their six chimes, Mona Sofia saw off her last client, a wealthy silk merchant. Climbing down the stairs of the brothel, the man wrapped himself in the woolen shawl he wore over his *lucco*, pulled his *beretta* over his eyebrows and, peering across the threshold, made sure that no-one saw him leave. From the brothel, he walked straight to the Holy Trinity whose bells were calling the faithful to early Mass.

Mona Sofia felt weary. Her back ached. To her annoyance,

[5] It should be noted that a thousand ducats was a fortune sufficient to live all one's life in the lap of luxury.

when she drew the purple silk curtains of her bedroom window, she saw that dawn had already risen. She hated having to fall asleep amid the bustle from outside, and she told herself that this was a good opportunity to take full advantage of the day. Reclining against the headboard of her bed, she started making plans. First she would dress like a lady and go to Mass at St Mark's Cathedral (the truth be told, it was quite a long time since she had been to Mass); she would go to confession and then, free of remorse, she would pay a visit to the Bottega del Moro to buy several perfumes which she had long promised herself. She went on making plans, drawing the blankets a little closer (after the tiring night, this first moment of rest had begun to muddle her thoughts) and she closed her eyes in order to think more clearly.

The bells had not yet stopped ringing when Mona Sofia, just as she did every morning, fell into a deep and placid sleep.

II

BOUT THE SAME TIME, BUT IN FLORENCE, A fine rain was falling on the bell tower of the modest Abbey of San Gabriele. The bells rang with such determination, one would have said a fat abbot and not a woman with delicate hands was pulling the ropes. With the punctual devotion that every morning drew her from her bed before dawn, in cold weather or hot, in rain or frost, Inés de Torremolinos swung from the ropes with her light frame and, as if the Almighty Himself were aiding her, she succeeded in swaying the bells whose weight was no less than a thousand times that of her feminine and immaculate body.

Inés de Torremolinos lived in Franciscan austerity in spite of being one of the wealthiest women in Florence. The eldest daughter of an aristocratic Spanish couple, she had been still very young when she was wedded to a distinguished Florentine lord. Following the rules of marriage, she left her native Castile to live in her husband's palazzo in Florence. Fate decreed that Inés was to become a widow without giving her husband a new link to continue his noble lineage: she gave birth to three daughters and not a single son.

As a young widow, all that Inés owned was this: the sorrow of not having given birth to a boy, a few olive groves, vineyards, castles, money, and a charitable and pious soul. Therefore, in order to forget her pain and mend her faults in memory of the departed, she decided to turn into cash all the property and goods she had inherited from her late husband (in Florence) and from her father (in Castile), and with this fortune build an abbey. In this way she would remain forever united with her lamented husband by means of a pure and celibate existence, and she would dedicate her life to the service of the male children her womb had been incapable of producing: in other words, the monastic community and the poor. And so she did.

One might have called Inés a happy woman. Her Franciscan eyes radiated peace and tranquility. Her words were an unending balm for the tormented. She consoled the disconsolate and she guided the lost sheep back on the right path. One would have said there were no obstacles on her road to sainthood.

On that dawn in 1558, at the same time as, in Venice, Mona Sofia was ending her exhausting and profitable night, Inés de Torremolinos was beginning her day of happy and charitable works. Neither woman had any knowledge of the remote existence of the other. Nothing would have led them to suppose that they had something in common. And yet fate at times carves a path through the impossible. Without the slightest suspicion of their destiny, without being aware of one another, each woman was to become a point of the same trinity whose apex was in Padua.

THE CROW

I

N THE HIGHEST SPOT OF THE MASSIVE CLIFF that separates Verona from Trento, on the last rock that juts out from the ring of hills that crowns the peak of Monte Veldo, quiet as the stone on which he perched, the profile of a crow outlined itself against the dusky horizon whose golden epicentre did not seem to come from the sun, still only a vague promise, but from the very gold of Venice, as if the foundations of that vault of light were the distant Byzantine domes of the Cathedral of St Mark. It was the hour that precedes the day. The crow was waiting. He was patient. And he had, as always, a voracious but not pressing hunger. His domain was all of Venice, Euganean Venice (Treviso, Rovigo, Verona and, further away, Vicenza) and also Julian Venice. But his roost was in Padua.

Down below, everything was ready for the feast of St Theodore, the *festa de tori*. After midday, the crowd, between drinks, would shackle five or six oxen, and, while as many women held their horns, they would slit the beasts' throats one by one, with a single and accurate stroke of the sword. It was as if the crow knew that this would happen. He could smell in advance his favorite smell. But he also knew that, even if he was lucky, he would be barely able to steal one miserable eyeball or piece of gut, for which he would have to fight with the dogs. It wasn't worth the distance, nor the risk, nor the effort.

Still he hadn't moved. He had the patience of crows. He could have waited until the Moors in the clock tower sounded the last stroke of the bell. Then, just as it did every morning, there would appear on the Grand Canal the public barge that collected the corpses from the Hospital on its way to the Cemetery Island. But this too would not be worth his while: with luck, all he might manage to tear away would be a morsel of foul meat, lean and ravaged by the plague.

He turned on his feet and looked in the opposite direction, eastwards, where he had his home. There was his master. Then the crow took wing toward Padua.

I I

HE CROW FLEW OVER THE CATHEDRAL'S TEN
domes and over the university. He perched
above the pediment of the fourth door leading
to the interior courtyard. He waited, knowing
that his master would come out any minute. It
happened every day. The crow was patient. He spread one of
his wings and dug his beak into his feathers. One might have
thought he paid no attention to anything except his own intimate pleasures, preening his chest, ridding himself of a flea.

Just as the bells began calling to Mass, the crow grew as tense
as a rope, then slowly unfolded his wings, gave a dull caw and
prepared himself to jump onto the shoulder of his master who,
every morning, would appear under the archway and, before
setting off for the parish church, would pass by the morgue to
give his crow that which he so enjoyed: a still warm piece of
tripe.

But on that winter's morning, things would not be as they
had always been. The first stroke of the bell sounded and the
crow's master had not yet appeared. The crow knew that his

master was inside the cloister; he could smell him, he could even hear him breathing. And still he did not come out. The crow cawed with annoyance. He was hungry.

The crow and his master were fully aware of each other and, for that very reason, held one another in a mutual and secret distrust. Leonardino (this was the name the master had given him) never settled quite fully on his master's shoulder; he kept a small distance between his feet and the stole, lifting himself off with a short and regular flapping of wings. Neither did the master trust his companion. Both of them, as they well knew, shared the same inquisitive spirit that led them to seek what lurks behind the flesh.

The second stroke of the bell was heard and still the master did not appear. Something strange was taking place, the crow could guess as much.

Every day, Leonardino, perched on the balustrade of the morgue's stairs, would attentively follow his master's movements, the knowledgeable hands guiding the scalpel; then, when he saw the blood surging behind the thin groove the blade left in its wake, Leonardino would rock from left to right and let out a caw of satisfaction.

Not for want of trying, his master had never succeeded in getting Leonardino to eat out of his hand. There certainly were good reasons for the crow to be afraid. Leonardino knew who had owned the tripe his master had offered him on the previous day; he had recognized the stench of the cat who, until yesterday, had sat trustingly in the man's lap; the man who, with the same hand that had patted it and fed it, had skilfully gutted the cat in order to dissect it.

'Leonardino,' the master would coo while slowly

approaching the crow with a bit of tripe in his hand.

'Leonardino,' he would repeat, and as he advanced a step further, the crow would retreat another step.

Leonardino did not look at the tripe; he could smell it, but he didn't look at it. He had his eyes glued on the eyes of his master, eyes which, apparently, seemed to him more appetizing than the morsel of gut. At length, the man would throw him the tripe and the crow would pounce on it with long-contained voracity.

But that morning no-one appeared under the archway. The third stroke of the bell was heard and the crow realized that his master would not keep their daily appointment. Disgusted and hungry, Leonardino set flight for Venice.

THE APEX

I

HE MASTER'S NAME WAS MATEO RENALDO Colombo and that winter's morning of 1558 he had good reason not to keep his habitual appointment with Leonardino. Locked in between four walls in his room at the University of Padua, Mateo Colombo was busy writing:

'If I have the right to give a name to the things I have discovered, I shall call this thing Love or the Pleasure of Venus,' he wrote, thereby concluding the statement he had been composing all night long. As he closed the thick vellum-bound notebook in which he had been writing, he heard the bells calling to Mass. He rubbed his red eyes; his back felt tired. He looked toward the small moon-shaped window above his desk and he realized that the candle next to the notebook was burning uselessly. Beyond, above the domes of the cathedral, the sun was beginning to warm the air and slowly to dry the dew that shone on the green lawn of the university. From the other side of the courtyard, the perfume wafted in of incense burning in the chapel, replaced from time to time, according to the whims of the wind, by the hospitable aromas of the smoky kitchen chimney. As the sun rose over the tiles of the archway, the warm bustling sounds from the Piazza dei Frutti also began to rise. The shouts of the shopkeepers and the cries of the wandering hawkers, the bleating of the sheep offered at two ducats, their price called out by the peasant women who herded them into the city, all rose in contrast with the monastic silence imposed by the bells calling to Mass.

Still sleepy, rubbing their hands against the cold and exhaling puffs of white breath, students poured out of the pavilions into the arched cloisters that surrounded the central courtyard, converging in a single file that made its way into the small atrium of the chapel.

Standing next to the parish priest, Alessandro di Legnano, dean of the university, unctuously watched over the orderly process, imposing silence with a mere look, sternly administered here and there, or even, when it became necessary, with a pointed clearing of the throat directed toward the lawbreakers.

Before the last stroke of the bell, Mateo Colombo stood up and walked to the door. Only when he turned the handle and realized that the door to his room had been locked from outside, did he remember that the bells were not ringing for him. The weariness of the night spent at work, but even more the force of habit, which every morning led him to the chapel after a brief visit to the morgue, had made him forget that today, by disposition of the Superior Tribunal, he was a prisoner in his own room. He felt a pang of guilt toward his Leonardino. Perhaps he should have felt thankful for his lot; no doubt it would have been worse to have landed in a cold and filthy cell in the San Antonio Prison. Perhaps he should have thanked the committee and the dean for not having thrown him in chains and for allowing him still to see the warm winter sun through the small moon-shaped window of his room. Certainly the charges against him called for the most rigorous punishment: heresy, perjury, blasphemy, witchcraft and satanism. Men were thrown into jail for far less. Even now, from his room, he could hear how the passersby jeered and spat at the prisoners exposed in the stocks on the piazza. And these were mere pilferers of trinkets . . .

The last few students passing under Mateo Colombo's window stood on their toes to look inside; the anatomist could hear the whispers and malicious laughter of those who, until yesterday, had been his own pupils, some of whom might even one day have become his faithful disciples. He could see them.

Even though he should have felt thankful for his lot, Mateo Colombo cursed the day on which he had left his native Cremona. He cursed the day his prosecutor, the dean, had decided to appoint him to the Chair of Anatomy and Surgery. And he cursed the day on which, forty-two years earlier, he had been born.

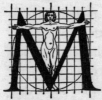ATEO RENALDO COLOMBO, *'IL CHIRURGO'* AS his fellow countrymen called him, or, in his Paduan exile, *'Il Cremonese'*, had studied pharmakopeia and surgery at the university where he was now held prisoner. He was first Leoniens's most brilliant disciple and later that of Vesalius. It was Vesalius himself who proposed to the dean, Alessandro di Legnano, that his Cremonese disciple be his successor to the chair when, in 1542, he left to teach in Germany and Spain. Still very young, Mateo Colombo earned in his own right the title of *Maestro dei Maestri*, Teacher of Teachers. It made Alessandro di Legnano proud that his Cremonese employee should have been the first to discover the laws of pulmonary circulation before the Englishman Harvey, who, most unjustly, would ultimately receive the laurels. Many had considered Mateo Colombo mad when he had declared that blood drew its oxygen from the lungs and that there were no orifices in the division between the two ventricles of the heart, thereby daring to refute Galen himself. And it was certainly a

dangerous proposition: one year earlier, Miguel de Servet had been forced to flee Spain when, in his *Christianismi Restitutio*, he declared that blood was the soul of the flesh, *anima ipsa est sanguins*; his attempt to explain in anatomical terms the doctrine of the Holy Trinity led him to the stake in Geneva, where he was burned on green wood 'to prolong his agony'.[6] But the laurels due to Mateo Colombo for his discovery were snatched up by the Englishman Harvey barely fifty years later – 'the only anatomist', according to Hobbes in *Dei Corpore*, 'to have seen his doctrine gain acceptance during his lifetime'.

Mateo Colombo was eminently a man of the Renaissance: a child of the arts, a product of finery and ornament, the prodigal son of that world in which everything, from the domes of the cathedrals to the glasses from which the peasants drank, from the frescoes that decorated the palaces to the sickles with which the farmhands reaped their harvest, from the arches of the churches to the shepherds' wooden staffs – everything was prodigiously crafted. From that same stuff was made Mateo Colombo's soul; it had the same ornamental gracefulness, the same amiable *gentilezza*. In those days everyone was infused with the spirit of Leonardo: the artisan was an artist, the artist a scientist, the scientist a warrior, and the warrior an artisan. Knowledge meant knowing how to make something with your own hands. And, as if there were not enough examples already, Pope Eugene I had used his own hands to cut off the head of a treasonous prefect.

With the same skill with which he used the pen in his

[6] Knut Haeger, *The Illustrated History of Surgery*, H. Starke, 1989.

vellum-bound notebook, Mateo Colombo handled brushes
and prepared paints with which he executed the most splendid
anatomical charts. Had he wished, he would have been capable
of painting like Luca Signorelli or like the great Michelangelo
himself. In his self-portrait, he presented himself as a man of
fine but imposing features, his black eyes and thick, dark beard
betraying perhaps a Moorish ancestry. The forehead, high and
prominent, is framed between parted hair that falls down to
his shoulders. His hands are pale and delicate and his long,
thin fingers lend him an almost feminine elegance. Between
the index and the thumb, he holds a scalpel. This self-portrait
is not only a faithful rendering of his physiognomy, but also
of his obsession: if one looks carefully (because it is quite
difficult to see) below the scalpel, in the lower section of the
painting, one can make out, in a sort of vague mist, the naked
and lifeless body of a woman. The painting brings to mind
that of a contemporary: Sebastiano del Piombo's *St Bernard*.
The disproportion that exists between the beatific expression
of the saint and the violent gesture as he pierces with his
staff the body of a demon, is the same that can be seen between
the anatomist's face and the act of sinking his scalpel into the
female flesh. His expression is one of triumph.

In an age of great names and extraordinary celebrities,
Mateo Colombo carried his own name like a millstone. How to
avoid the weighty shadow cast upon him by his illustrious
Genoese namesake? Mateo Colombo was condemned to
parody, and to the easy mockery of his detractors.

His work was certainly no less extraordinary than that of the
other Colombo. He too discovered his America, he too had his
share of both glory and unhappiness. And he also knew how to

be cruel. Mateo Colombo, when the time came to establish his *colonia*, his colony, had no more scruples or pity than Christopher. The shaft of his banner would not be sunk into the warm sands of the Tropics, but into the core of the newly discovered land which he had claimed for himself: the female body.

III

PRISONER IN HIS OWN CELL, MATEO Colombo had just finished writing the statement that he was to present to the court. The echo of the last bell calling to Mass was still reverberating when he saw, outside his window, a figure with his back to the light.

'May I be of assistance?' murmured the figure.

Mateo Colombo, who, under orders of the court, had been forced to take a vow of silence, cautiously declined to speak but drew a little nearer. Only then could he make out who it was standing against the sun: his friend, Messer Vittorio.

'Are you mad, do you wish to end up in jail like myself?' he whispered and with an inhospitable gesture urged him to leave at once.

Messer Vittorio put a hand through the bars of the window and offered his friend a skin of goat's milk and a sackful of bread. With annoyance, as if against his will, Mateo Colombo took both. He was certainly hungry. As the furtive visitor turned to go back to the chapel, he heard the prisoner whisper:

'Can you send a letter for me, by messenger, to Florence?'

Messer Vittorio hesitated.

'You could have asked for something easier. You know how zealously the dean rifles through all correspondence . . .' Just then, both men saw Alessandro di Legnano standing at the chapel door, making certain that everybody was attending Mass.

'Fine, give me the letter. Now I must go,' said Messer Vittorio urgently, reaching with his hand between the bars.

'I have not written it yet. If you could come by after Mass . . .'

Then the dean spotted Messer Vittorio under the archway.

'What are you doing there?' he asked, arms akimbo, his frown deeper than usual.

Messer Vittorio bent to pull at the laces of his sandal, then walked toward the chapel.

'Were you speaking to your shoe?'

Messer Vittorio merely blushed and grinned stupidly.

Mateo Colombo had only the short duration of the Mass to write his letter.

After checking that there was no-one outside the chapel, he again pulled out his notebook, which he kept hidden under the small desk, since he had been forbidden to communicate with anyone; took a goose's quill, dipped it in the inkwell and, on the last page, set himself to work. The vow of silence imposed by the tribunal was not an arbitrary punishment; it had a very specific objective: to prevent his satanic discovery from spreading like seeds in the wind. For that reason, he had been forbidden to write. There was not much time left. Once again he made sure that there was no-one near. Then he began:

My lady,

*My soul is struggling in an abyss of uncertainty, oppressed by
the bitterness of him who, having sworn secrecy in the Name
of the Lord, gives offence to the Holy Name when, unjustly,
one tiny part of His Divine Creation is kept hidden from our
eyes. It is therefore in the Name of God, my beloved Inés,
that I have decided to break the vows of silence imposed upon
me by the dean of the University of Padua and by the Doctors
of the Church. I fear death less than I fear silence, even
though, in my case, I am condemned both to one and to the
other. When this letter reaches you in Florence, I will no
longer be alive. I have spent the night writing out the statement that tomorrow I am to present to the court over which
Cardinal Caraffa will preside. And yet, I know full well that
before I pronounce a single word in my defense, the sentence
will have long been decided. I know that no other fate awaits
me but the fire at the stake. If I felt that you might be suc-
cessful in interceding for my life in this mockery of a trial,
undoubtedly I would ask you to do so: many things have I
asked of you; one more will not matter. But I also know that
my fate is cast. All I ask from you now is that you hear me
out. That is all.*

*You may wonder perhaps why I have decided to reveal my
secret to you alone. It happens that, even though you did not
know it, you were the single source of the discoveries that were
granted to me. All depends on you now. Should you consider
that I am committing a sacrilege by speaking out when I have
sworn to keep silent, stop reading now and throw these papers*

into the flames. If, however, I still deserve some credit in your eyes and you decide to read on, I pray you, in the Name of God Himself, to keep the secret.

Before proceeding with the letter, Mateo Colombo sat in doubt for a few moments. Time grew short. Mass would be half over. He rubbed his eyes, turned in his chair and, before continuing, asked himself whether this was not all madness.

This was the beginning of the tragedy. Had he known that what he was about to reveal to Inés de Torremolinos would result in something worse than either death or silence, he would not have written one more word. As it was, he once again dipped the quill in the inkwell.

He had just finished his letter when he saw that the congregation had begun to leave the chapel.

Mateo Colombo tore the page from the notebook and folded it in such a way that only the blank side remained visible. The students were the first to emerge and, from the centre of the courtyard, they began to move in small groups toward the classrooms. Last of all, Messer Vittorio appeared and, by his side, Alessandro di Legnano. Messer Vittorio stopped in the atrium and with a nod of his head, bid the dean farewell. Mateo Colombo, through the window of his cell, saw the dean standing next to his friend and showing no inclination to move. He saw that the dean, leaning now against a column, had begun one of his usual interrogations. He wasn't able to hear what they were saying, but the anatomist was quite familiar with Alessandro di Legnano's inquisitorial gestures, scowling, with his hands on his hips.

The anatomist had lost all hope of giving his friend the letter, when suddenly the dean walked away toward his own rooms. Messer Vittorio stayed on a while longer and, when he saw that there was no-one left in the courtyard or skulking under the archway, he walked quickly and directly up to the anatomist's window. Mateo Colombo threw his letter through the bars. Messer Vittorio nudged the letter with his foot until it seemed far enough, then he bent over and placed it between the heel and the sole of his sandal. At that very moment, Alessandro di Legnano reappeared at the far end of the archway.

'It seems to be time for you to replace your footwear,' said the dean. And before Messer Vittorio was able to think of an answer, Alessandro di Legnano added:

'I will see you in the workshop.' He spun round on his heels and returned the way he had come.

Messer Vittorio wished the dean dead; a wish that, in a certain sense, he would one day see granted.

THE DEAN

I

LESSANDRO DI LEGNANO'S HEAD WAS LYING on Messer Vittorio's table, with its eyes fixed on the ceiling of the workshop – 'fixed' being a mere turn of phrase because, in fact, the eyes were two dead spheres. The artist rubbed his hand over the dean's head, which looked as if it had been cut from the body, stopped above the wrinkled frown, steadied his chisel and landed a dry, dull blow of the mallet that raised a cloud of dust like the dust of bones. The dean was deadly stiff but his expression was very much alive. He was, however, cold as ice. Colder, in fact, than a corpse. It had taken Messer Vittorio half a year to complete the bust of Alessandro di Legnano, who now rose from the bench on which he had sat posing and walked up to the sculpture he had commanded in his honor. He observed himself, nose against nose, and one might have said that he was staring at a mirror made of Carrara marble. The artist had succeeded in copying his client's exact expression and anyone stopping to inspect the bust would have felt the same repugnance that people felt when facing the dean

himself. This was exactly what had happened to Messer Vittorio during the last six months of work – and it was not lack of desire that stopped him from sinking his chisel into the forehead of the dean himself, especially after hearing his verdict:

'I have seen worse things,' Alessandro di Legnano said, while inspecting himself somewhat scornfully and practically throwing the fifteen ducats into Messer Vittorio's face.

'Let it be brought to my office this afternoon,' he added as he turned and left the workshop, slamming the door.

The bust Messer Vittorio had just finished was faithful to its model. It might have been said that the dean had the expression of a perfect idiot: swollen features, a severe prognathism that held up the face above a sort of maxillary balcony, and half-closed eyelids that lent it a somnolent look. The Florentine craftsman had not been kind; if he liked his clients, he was generous enough to embellish them a little, as he had done, for instance, with the irredeemable profile of a certain illustrious personage close to the Medici family. But Alessandro di Legnano's bust was the embodiment of Messer Vittorio's opinion of Alessandro di Legnano.

No-one in the whole of Padua liked the dean. And no-one would have felt sorry to see him dead.

As he did every morning, close to the stroke of midday, Alessandro di Legnano set off to visit the Piazza dei Frutti. He would cross the Riviera de San Benedetto, he would be greeted with exaggerated politeness by all passersby and, after turning toward the Ponte Tadi, the same passersby would wish him all sorts of misfortunes under their breath. The fat fruit-vendor from whom the dean would daily buy a few apricots, wished him the best of health and, echoing Messer Vittorio's secret hopes, would pray under her breath that her customer choke on a stone. And the tailor, at whose store the dean would stop to order a *lucco* of silk, prayed to see him hanged in the delicate stole he had ordered the previous week and which the dean now appraised with a grimace of disgust, saying:

'Did you happen to cut this with your teeth?'

Alessandro di Legnano knew that everyone hated him. And the knowledge gave him immense pleasure.

The dean had been the disciple of Jacob Sylvius of Paris, but he was certainly not as gifted as his teacher in the medical arts. All that Alessandro di Legnano had inherited from Sylvius was a visceral tendency to awaken contempt in his fellow human beings. The slew of adjectives once applied to the French anatomist – miserly, ill-mannered, arrogant, resentful, cynical and greedy, among others – was too weak to describe the dean of Padua University. And he himself did not expect as his epitaph a less damning one than that which had been composed in memory of his teacher:

> *Here lies Sylvius who in life*
> *Never stirred but for a fee.*
> *Dead, he rages, in the knowledge*
> *You can read these lines for free.*

I I

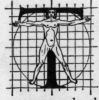HAT MORNING THE DEAN WAS IN AN excellent mood. He seemed fully at ease. He wore the spiritual look of one who has been victorious in battle. And that is exactly what he had been. Now he was anticipating, somewhat prematurely, the delights of a much longed-for bonfire that, if it were up to him, he would gladly light with his own hands. He was anxiously waiting for the dawning day to come to an end. Tomorrow would see the beginning of the trial for which he had pleaded, not without innumerable obstacles, in the presence of the cardinals Caraffa and Alvarez de Toledo and, finally, before Pope Paul III himself.

Alessandro di Legnano was full of animation, striding out as if suddenly he had left behind the gout which he had been dragging along for years like a persistent dead weight. His euphoria was so great that he had not even noticed that a piece of badly folded paper was sticking out from Messer Vittorio's sandal. Perhaps Messer Vittorio's solicitousness was due to simple ignorance. Perhaps the Florentine sculptor was unaware that, if he were to be discovered talking to the anatomist, he would suffer the same fate as his friend. Because, according to the Holy Legislature, whoever spoke to one accused of heresy was regarded as an heretic himself.

Mateo Colombo had become the dean's lasting obsession. The two men had never liked each other. Alessandro di Legnano bore toward Mateo Colombo a hatred that owed much to the admiration he subconsciously felt for him. He had always addressed the anatomist disdainfully and missed no opportunity to disparage him in front of the students, calling him *il barbiere*, the barber, in reference to the rule that excluded surgeons from the Royal College of Medicine, forcing them to join the Barbers' Guild and putting them on a par with bakers, brewers and public attorneys. Of course, once Mateo Colombo had become an eminence, the dean did not distance himself from the deluge of praise, and was happy to appropriate the congratulations that poured in from all parts of the world when the teacher under his command discovered the laws of the circulation of the blood, as if Mateo Colombo's achievements were attributable to the inspiration gleaned from his deanship.

The anatomist and the dean never felt affection for one another. On the contrary, they felt a reciprocal if not symmetrical envy. Mateo Colombo was the most respected anatomist in Europe; he enjoyed fame but not power. The dean, as everyone knew, even the Doctors of the Church, possessed an intelligence barely superior to that of a mule but he enjoyed a certain influence in the Vatican and boasted of the benediction of Pope Paul III. He had authority and a fair reputation among certain Inquisitors, for whom he had borne witness at more than one trial in which an heretical colleague had been condemned to the stake.

In the eyes of the dean, the anatomist's newest findings had exceeded all the limits of tolerance. The *Amor Veneris*, Mateo Colombo's America, went far beyond what was deemed permissible for science. For more than one reason, the mere mention of a certain 'pleasure of Venus' made the dean's gorge rise.

According to the dean, ever since the day on which Mateo Colombo had been appointed to the Chair of Surgery, the university had been transformed into a brothel that attracted peasants, courtesans, and, it was rumored, even Sisters of the Holy Orders, who entered the university by night and left before dawn. And all these women, rumor had it, left the anatomist's quarters with wide staring eyes and a smile like that of the Mona Lisa. As if this were not enough, he had heard that the whores of the Taverna del Mulo also frequented the anatomist's cell. And in this he was not mistaken.

INCE THE PAPAL BULL OF BONIFACE VIII had forbidden the dissection of cadavers, obtaining corpses was a job fraught with danger. And yet, in those days, there was in Padua a sort of black market of the dead. Its most solvent member was a certain Giuliano Batista who, after a fashion, had come to put things in order in this free-for-all economy. During the time of the reckless Marco Antonio della Torre, the previous Professor of Anatomy, the students had been encouraged to open graves, rifle the hospital morgues, and even take down the condemned from their cautionary gibbets. In fact, their teacher barely prevented them from murdering those who walked the streets at night. Such was their zeal that they were even forced to take precautions against one another. Such was their necrophilia that the highest compliment to which a woman could aspire in their hands was 'What a beautiful body', before they proceeded to cut her throat.

By contrast, their earliest predecessor, Mundini dei Luzzi,

who two hundred and fifty years earlier had conducted
the first public anatomical dissection of two cadavers at the
university of Bologna, had been possessed of a fine sense of
decorum which had prevented him from opening up the head,
'the dwelling of the soul and of reason'.

Giuliano Batista had the monopoly of the cadaver market.
He would buy them from needy relatives, hangmen and
gravediggers and, after restoring them to a presentable condition, he would sell them to university students, professors and
respectable necrophiles.

He knew, nevertheless, that in the case of Mateo Colombo
there was no need to prettify the merchandise: you can't fool
an anatomist. So Batista was spared the effort of applying
rouge to the dead cheeks, and of bringing back the shine of the
eyes with turpentine, and the gloss of the nails with varnish
from across the seas.

If the anatomist required, for example, to examine a liver,
Giuliano Batista would pull out the organ, fill the vacant
compartment with tow or rags, put aside the goods, sew up the
cadaver with a silken thread, and sell the body to another
client. If a corpse was beyond repair, Giuliano Batista would
find a market for the separate parts. Nothing went to waste:
the hair to the Guild of Barbers and the teeth to the Guild of
Goldsmiths.

The dissection of cadavers was both commonplace and
illegal, but everyone knew that Pope Boniface VIII's Bull
carried, in practice, no force whatsoever. And yet the only one
on whom the dean imposed the ban was Mateo Colombo. The
anatomist knew that Alessandro di Legnano looked the other
way in everyone else's case, even in the case of his students;

Mateo Colombo was the only exception and he was therefore obliged to proceed with the greatest of care.

In recent times, Mateo Colombo had bought close to ten cadavers, all belonging to women. He compiled scrupulous catalogs on the dissected corpses in which he recorded name, age, cause of death, together with a description and drawings, not only of the examined organs but also of the expression on each face.

But his methods seemed more suitable for living flesh than dead, and for one piece of flesh in particular, one which was hardly ever found behind university doors because it was forbidden – forbidden by the dean with more scruples than success. The statutes of the university clearly forbade the entry of women. However, for reasons less related to the business of science than to the impetuosity of hot blood, there were frequent and furtive female visits, peasant girls from the farms nearby who, from time to time, would offer doctors and students a night of joy.

One of the ways of gaining access to the university, other than climbing the high walls, was to hide among the corpses that, once a week, were brought, on a public cart, to the morgue. There, hidden under a shroud, the women would remain motionless until left alone in the cellars from where their lovers would collect them.

Once, perhaps impatient after a long and enforced conti-nence, a certain famous doctor undressed one of these peasant girls right in the middle of the morgue, among the dead, and, in the very moment of a glorious fellatio, the university priest walked into the cellar. He saw a body, which he had seen being delivered as a corpse, now rocking backward and forward. The

illustrious doctor did not immediately perceive the presence
of the priest who, spellbound, stared at the doctor's thin
legs and at the not-so-thin member as it showered the well-
proportioned 'corpse'. When, after a last quiver, the doctor
finally noticed the priest standing at the door, he just managed
to shout, with an exorbitant grimace: '*Miracolo! Miracolo!*'
And without drawing breath, he began to lecture on the
Aristotelian theories concerning the humors carried by
the semen which, according to the metaphysician, was the true
source of life. And why would it not be possible, if semen was
capable of creating life, for it to bring back the dead to the
world of the living? All this he said while tucking away his still
somewhat tumescent member. As he ended his feverish solil-
oquy, the doctor ran out through the door and up the stairs
shouting, '*Miracolo! Miracolo!*'

The truth is that Mateo Colombo had his own reasons for
bringing women into the university. And the women who
secretly visited the anatomist also had reasons of their own.

The hands of Mateo Colombo had learned to touch a woman's
body, much as the hands of a musician learn to touch an instrument. He had crossed the vague boundary that separates
science from art and had taught his hands to touch the most
sublime, the most elevated and most difficult of instruments.
His art was the ephemeral art of giving pleasure, a discipline
that, like conversation, leaves neither trace nor record.

I V

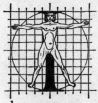T WAS MIDDAY WHEN MESSER VITTORIO left the university and headed in the direction of the piazza. Under the warm winter sun, street performers, surrounded by a crowd of casual onlookers, were attempting to build a human tower which they then deliberately collapsed. Further ahead, at the far end of the piazza, a group of austere men, shopkeepers and *signori* , formed a circle around the *banditori* who took turns to read out the day's proclamations. A few steps further were those who preferred to consult the travelers arriving from beyond Monte Veldo, bringing news either true or false, but certainly more interesting than the local edicts.

Messer Vittorio was walking quickly. He passed the three sets of stocks where the day's thieves were exhibited, squeezing through the throng of old women and young girls who were competing to spit on the poor wretches. At the other end of the piazza, the last departing messenger closed his saddlebags and was on the point of mounting his horse.

Nervously, Messer Vittorio stopped to listen to the latest news from the *banditori*. He couldn't prevent a horrible prickling down his neck as he passed by the stocks again. If the weather held, in less than a month the letter would reach Florence. By then, except for a miracle, Mateo Colombo would be dead.

Fate decreed that the weather would hold.

THE NORTH

I

ATEO COLOMBO'S CELL WAS A PERFECT cube. The small moon-shaped window above had no pane of glass in it. In fact, the only windows in the university that did have glass were those in the deanery and the lecture hall. Though glass was certainly functional, above all in winter, it smacked of bad taste to place it next to the exquisite Venetian silks that covered each and every opening. It was easy to recognize the houses of the nouveaux riches in Padua: they all had windows protected by painted glass. But the window in Mateo Colombo's cell lacked even a plain silk covering. Its only protection was a piece of ordinary cloth that stopped the wind at the cost of barring even the faintest ray of light. If the anatomist did not want to remain in the dark, he had to suffer drafts, cold and, if it was raining, damp. The cell was divided in two by a bookshelf that rose to the murky heights of the ceiling. The back of the cell served as the bedroom: a wooden bed with no canopy and, next to it, a night table and a candlestick. In the other half, opposite the set of shelves and

against the outside wall, was the small desk. Whoever came in from the archway could see a desk flanked by a set of shelves that held an infinity of strange embalmed beasts, fierce enough to dissuade an incautious thief from entering.

Since his imprisonment, Mateo Colombo would spend most of his time staring through the bars of his window. He was there, his eyes lost in the distance, when he saw Messer Vittorio passing the main door. With the slightest gesture, the sculptor signaled to his friend that he had fulfilled the dangerous errand. Mateo Colombo gave a deep sigh of relief; his fate, already decided, worried him less than that of Messer Vittorio.

The anatomist did not expect for himself the clemency shown to his teacher, Vesalio, when he had been sent to the Tribunal of the Holy Office. On one occasion, Andrea Vesalio had confessed to Mateo Colombo a shameful and unfortunate event that had almost led him to the stake: he had asked permission to dissect a young Spanish nobleman who had died during a consultation. After having obtained the agreement of the dead man's parents, he opened up the breast and, to his astonished despair, he saw that the heart was still beating. Told of this, the parents accused Vesalio of murder and began proceedings against him at the Holy Office. The Inquisition condemned him to death; however, shortly before the fires were lit, the King of Spain himself intervened, deciding to commute Vesalio's sentence and ordering instead that the anatomist go on a pilgrimage to the Holy Land to cleanse himself of his crime.

Mateo Colombo knew that his 'crime' was infinitely more serious, since it consisted in having unveiled that which should have been left hidden forever. Therefore he held no hope, not even if he were to retract his discovery as another graduate of Padua had done, the famous Galileo Galilei. In any case, Galileo's discovery was, in practical terms, too intangible to appear as a serious threat. His own America, on the other hand, was within the reach of any fool.

'What would become of mankind if the Devil's hosts were to take hold of your discovery?' the dean had said after the disclosure, when he imposed on Mateo Colombo a vow of silence and suggested, at the same time, that the discoverer himself had joined the ever-increasing ranks of the Devil's party.

'What misfortune would not fall upon mankind if Evil were to hold sway over the will of the female flock?' the dean had said, suggesting that his purpose had been to possess that female will himself, in the name of doing good.

Therefore Mateo Colombo could expect no other fate than death at the stake.

And yet, there was another cause for the tightness in his throat: not the certainty of imminent death, nor his captivity, not even the imposition of silence. Neither was it the memory of Inés de Torremolinos nor the uncertain fate of the letter he had written her. Nor was it the broken vow of silence he had sworn to keep. What tortured him was not the sorrow of being unable to make public his discovery, but rather that he had failed in the innocent purpose which had led him on his quest.

The compass north that had led Mateo Colombo to his discovery was not a theological premise, as he had claimed, nor the ambition for philosophical knowledge which he had cited in support of his claim, nor even a desire to revolutionize anatomy as, to his sorrow, he had indeed succeeded in doing. He would not walk resolutely into the flames in the name of Truth, as his colleague Tomà Miguel de Servet had done.

The starting-point of his discovery was nothing other than thwarted love. He did not wish for an understanding of the general laws that govern the dark ways of women but only, barely, for a place in one specific woman's heart.

The compass north that had led Mateo Colombo to his new-found-land had a name: Mona Sofia.

LA PUTTANA

I

ONA SOFIA WAS BORN ON THE ISLAND OF Corsica. She was not yet two months old when she was stolen from her mother's side one summer's morning, while she was doing the washing in a brook that led into the sea. The island of Corsica was, at the time, the place least suited for a woman to give birth to a beautiful child. Since first Mark Anthony, and later Pompey, had evicted the Cilician pirates from the Republic, these Cilicians, after a long diaspora on the seas of Europe and Asia Minor, had founded a new homeland with patient and brutal obstinacy, this time on the islands of Corsica and Sardinia. It is said that because of her early promise of beauty, the pirates of Gorgar the Black took the baby on board, together with a group of Mongolian slaves, and sold her to a Greek trader. The baby girl survived the journey thanks to the care of a young slave whose son had been torn away from her and who still had a little milk left in her breasts. Her stay in

Greece was brief; a Venetian merchant bought her for a few ducats and once again took her on board, this time bound for Venice. The merchant already had a buyer lined up back home.

II

ONNA SIDONNA PAID TWENTY FLORINS FOR the child, convinced that she was making an excellent purchase. The first thing Donna Sidonna did, on receiving the infant black with filth, was to bathe her in a warm infusion of aromatic herbs. Then she rubbed her gums with a mixture of wine, water and honey, shaved her head, because her long locks had become as hard as wire, and finally placed her on a goatskin blanket close to the fire. When the child was fast asleep, Donna Sidonna fitted around her wrist the gold and ivory bracelet that was the trademark of all the novices of her house. And seeing that the infant one was thin and evidently anemic (on the ship she had been fed by the gaunt breast of a slave barely able to keep herself alive), Donna Sidonna appointed Oliva as the child's wet-nurse. Oliva was a young Egyptian slave with good and nourishing milk. She was called Oliva because of her olive-colored skin and because she was as tall as an olive tree. Oliva possessed all the assets of the perfect nurse. She was a slender woman with majestic breasts and

nipples the size of a gold florin. Among other features, she was dark-haired, and it was known that blonde women produced a bitter and watery milk. After a week some improvement was already visible; the child started to display healthy baby fat and would burp with the strength of an adult. Her stools, punctiliously examined by Donna Sidonna herself, were firm and of a color that revealed the perfect functioning of her bowels.

The first month after the child's arrival, Donna Sidonna wrapped her in a dress rich with lace, perfumed her with jasmine water and called for the priest to give the child her first sacrament, because a good whore must be a Christian. As she had so many times before, Donna Sidonna haggled over the price of the Holy Offices; finally the sum was agreed. The priest had demanded the favors of one of the novices every day for a month and '*per tutti gli orifizi*'. Donna Sidonna had offered the service for a week only and it included no favors beyond the conventional 'Franciscan' position. They finally agreed that the priest would enjoy the novice's services for fifteen days and '*per tutti gli orifizi*'. On that very same morning the child was baptized and Donna Sidonna gave her the name of Ninna.

Ninna shared the house with eight other baby girls in the same condition, but from very early on she began to show remarkable differences. None of the others cried so vehemently or ate with such appetite, so much so that Oliva's nipples were black and blue after every feed. And, unlike the others, Ninna obstinately resisted the swaddling clothes in which Donna Sidonna wrapped her charges every night to avoid grotesque deformities. So loud was the bawling with which the child announced her refusal that, as if infected, the others would become her chorus, like professional mourners echoing the weeping of the widow. This was the first innocent sign of dangerous rebellion. A good whore, like a good wife, had to be meek, obedient and grateful.

As the child grew in age, height and beauty, in the same proportion her character became more and more fiery. Her green almond-shaped eyes grew long, curved black lashes, but her gaze revealed a malicious and sarcastic cunning that inspired the same fear and fascination as a serpent's look inspires in its victims. In superstitious souls she awoke terror and a dread of evil omens. In religious spirits, she evoked satanic fears, because it was known that intelligence in a beautiful woman is an indubitable sign of demonic influence.

Shortly before her first birthday, Ninna began to mumble her first words which were, astonishingly, very different from the words the others were haltingly trying to mouth. While the other infant novices began to call their wet-nurses by their names and, as an early sign of gratitude, started to address Donna Sidonna as *Mamma*, Ninna would systematically ignore the presence of her benefactress and would not even deign to look at her. Useless were the efforts of the nurses who would hold her up to her *Mamma*, urging her, at the very least, to smile. It was no good; the most they would obtain from her was a healthy burp in the face of her protectress. Donna Sidonna would console herself with the thought that Ninna was still too young to understand her high destiny, the highest to which a woman dare aspire. These young girls could not yet appreciate what fortunes she was investing in each and every one of them; after all, Donna Sidonna was simply unburdening their parents from the misery of bringing a female child into the world. Though little Ninna's parents must have suffered when their daughter was stolen from them, it was best that they should have suffered once rather than have the pain dragged out for the rest of their lives. Surely they should be grateful to her. Who in their right mind could be happy with a daughter? Nothing but a drain on their resources during her unmarried years and, if by luck they managed to obtain a husband for her, there was still the payment of the dowry to consider. If everyone followed her example (thought Donna Sidonna), the money-lenders at the Dowry Bank would lose their profit from poor despairing fathers. Yet this was how the child thanked her: with crafty regurgitations and loud rebuffs from her nether end.

One morning, when Donna Sidonna had gone to scrutinize the sleep of her *figlia*, she found the girl standing in her cot and staring at her unflinchingly. To Donna Sidonna's great astonishment, Ninna greeted her as follows:

'*Puttana*,' she said with perfect pronunciation, and then added, 'give me ten ducats.'

These were Ninna's first five words. Donna Sidonna made the sign of the cross. Her first impulse was to run out of the room but such was her shock that all she could manage was to shout for help. There and then, Donna Sidonna decided that Ninna's five words were an incontrovertible sign that the child was possessed by the Devil. She decided to employ drastic measures.

Long before her nipples had bloomed, long before they had become as hard as a nut and of the diameter and texture of a petal, Ninna was sold to a tradesman for ten ducats, half what her benefactress had paid for her. One summer's morning she was put on sale in the public square with a group of Moorish slaves and young whores, and finally sold by her weight to a certain Madonna Creta, a philanthropic soul who, among other things, owned a brothel in Venice.

III

NINNA, WHOSE NAME WAS ENGRAVED ON her bracelet, was rebaptized with the more elegant name of Ninna Sofia. She was the brothel's youngest novice. Her new *mamma* was Madonna Creta, a prosperous and now retired courtesan. From Madonna Creta she could expect neither the sweetness nor the dedication bestowed upon her by her previous owner. And certainly no patience. The first time she lifted the child in her arms, Madonna Creta examined her as if she were a head of lettuce. She congratulated herself on her new purchase and calculated that, in barely a few years, two or three perhaps, her small investment might begin to yield returns. Venice suffered from a surplus of three things: noblemen, priests and pedophiles, and, of course, all possible combinations of these three. Yes, she said to herself, this was a bargain. She could see the face of Messer Girolamo di Benedetto discovering this young and still immaculate flesh; what would he not pay for the privilege of stroking with his decrepit fingers the furled vulva; what would he not give for the joy of rubbing his withered member against the plump thighs of the young novice. Madonna Creta could already count her golden ducats. But it was not going to be so easy.

Ninna Sofia examined the new bedroom she was to share with four adult novices. It was worse than a stable and, in fact, it reeked like a manger. It was a square room without a single window. Against the walls were wooden cots with straw bundles instead of mattresses, on which her new companions were seated, all slaves who had been bought for a handful of ducats. One had no teeth, another displayed the ravages of fairly advanced syphilis, and the other two had their eyes fixed on nothing. They all looked utterly defeated, touched with that sadness that lingers on until death, never far away. The air inside the room was warm and stifling. Ninna Sofia declared her dissatisfaction with a scream followed by shrill crying. When the door opened, Ninna, who was expecting the diligent arrival of Oliva, barely had time to see Madonna Creta advancing toward her. After the first three blows, she gathered that if she stopped crying, the punishment might cease. And so it did. At that very moment, little Ninna swore to herself never to cry again in her entire life. And so it was to be.

Her spirit became more and more unruly, more resilient and more dangerous. Ninna Sofia was like a poisonous flower.

Useless were the exemplary punishments which, lovingly and for her own good, of course, Madonna Creta bestowed upon her. Useless were the lashes that fell upon the girl's shoulders, the nightly penances of kneeling on kernels of corn, the promised circles of Hell. Ninna Sofia would stare at her

tutor through green eyes and heavy lashes, full of cunning
and malice. With a Gioconda smile, she would stare at her
tormentor with dry eyes and whisper:

'Have you finished, Madonna Creta?'

Madonna Creta decided that, if the girl was sufficiently
grown-up to ignore her lessons, she was also sufficiently
grown-up to earn her keep. Therefore, earlier than she had
planned, she went to pay a call on Messer Girolamo di
Benedetto and informed him of her new acquisition.

Messer Girolamo was one of the most prosperous silk
manufacturers of Venice and, until the previous year, he had
been Prior of the Guild. Since he was now an old man, he
had decided to withdraw from public duties, give himself over
entirely to a life of leisure, and begin to enjoy the few years still
left to him. In actual fact, he had never done anything else, only
now, instead of playing cards with his colleagues at the Guild,
he did so in his more comfortable palazzo. Messer Girolamo
di Benedetto had two weaknesses: card games and children. Of
course, he would never have tolerated being called a pedophile.
After all, what was wrong with a fondness for children, especially if he could help them financially, and even more
especially if the child's parents were poor?

The price demanded by Madonna Creta seemed to him
excessive, but he did not object; he had money in plenty and,
if he decided to spend it all in the years he had left, why not?
And even though he still enjoyed his old bargaining habits, in
these delicate matters he preferred to pay full price. He simply
requested from Madonna Creta a detailed description of the
girl. Messer Girolamo di Benedetto listened carefully, lost in

thought, and seemed to be enjoying himself in advance of the purchase. Had he known what little Ninna had in store for him, Messer Girolamo di Benedetto would no doubt have preferred to drop dead on the spot.

ESSER GIROLAMO DI BENEDETTO ARRIVED at the brothel at the hour agreed with Madonna Creta, an hour at which he could enter without being seen. He waited for a few strollers to turn the corner and at one point he even had to stop at the entrance of a store to allow a couple of women to finish their chatter a few steps away from the brothel's door. After they had said their farewells, he waited a few moments more, drew his hat over his face and finally, with a quick step, entered the small atrium.

With an unconsciously contemptuous gesture, Messer Girolamo di Benedetto refused the glass of wine that Madonna Creta offered him. He wanted to get down to business as soon as possible. His wizened heart was now beating with sudden youthful vigour. Such opportunities did not come daily. His love for small children had brought him many a headache; twice he had been publicly accused of child-molesting and, in spite of fortunately having been able to dissuade his accusers from going to court by means of heavy payments, there was much talk in Venice about the nature of Messer Girolamo di Benedetto's tastes. Madonna Creta, on the other hand, guaranteed silence. Her business demanded discretion. For that reason, he felt almost no regret about paying the twenty ducats they had agreed on.

Madonna Creta led him to the bedroom she had made ready for the occasion. Standing at the door, she invited Messer Girolamo to enter and, before leaving him alone with the little girl, said to him kindly:

'Enjoy yourself, but be careful not to hurt her.'

When Messer Girolamo di Benedetto first saw little Ninna, his eyes lit up. It was like a dream, to see her lying there, completely naked, on her stomach. The first thing Messer Girolamo did was to give her a few soft pats on the buttocks and drag his withered and bony fingers over her plump thighs. He let a thread of thick spittle fall on the child's back and spread it with his hand. Ninna showed no resistance and even smiled tenderly when the old man, in complete ecstasy, sat her on his lap. It had been many years since Messer Girolamo di Benedetto had enjoyed an erection and, as soon as he noticed this much longed-for event, he said to himself that little Ninna had performed a true miracle. Of course, it was not one of those erections of which he had been able to brag in his youth but it was better than nothing. He grabbed the child under her arms, lifted her up high and then placed her tiny buttocks over his member which now formed a modest promontory under the woolen *lucco* he was still wearing. He hadn't felt so aroused in a long time. Ninna, when she discovered the protuberance on which she was sitting, rubbed herself against it like a cat. This aroused the old man even more so that he impatiently lifted the *lucco* high above his belly and, holding his member in one hand, exhibited it to the child. Ninna examined the purplish object and immediately stretched her hand toward it. So small was Ninna's hand that she could barely grasp it.

'Are you not going to give my friend a kiss?' said the old man to Ninna who apparently thought it amusing that her client should thus address the purple thing and smiled in a manner the old man found frankly lascivious. That was the right word, 'lascivious'. Never before had he seen such a lustful disposition in a child. If an intruder had witnessed the scene, he would certainly have thought that little Ninna was guilty of abusing an old man! Just as Messer Girolamo di Benedetto had asked her, Ninna brought her mouth down to her client's member now hard and completely erect, more than it had ever been, even in the days of his youth. She kissed it with her lips, just as her wet-nurse Oliva had urged her to kiss Donna Sidonna's cheeks, although that was something she had always refused to do. Just like a grown-up woman, Ninna closed her eyes and moved her lips. The old man's eyes rolled up so that only the whites could be seen, and he trembled like a leaf. As if instead of having been nursed from the breast she had always been fed with male milk (though no-one had taught her the art of fellatio) Ninna opened her mouth as far as the corners of her lips would allow and almost swallowed the whole thing. The old man could not believe it.

'Little slut,' he muttered, 'little daughter of seven generations of sluts.'

And while he spoke, the child looked up at him with her green and long-lashed eyes, and swallowed the member even further. At that point, Ninna felt a throbbing in her mouth.

With all the strength of her jaw, she dug her teeth in, down to her gums, and then let herself fall from the bed. For a moment, Ninna remained in the air, hanging by her lips from the old man until, at last, she fell to the floor. Messer Girolamo di Benedetto, at first unable to understand, finally saw the fountain of blood gushing from his severed member. Only then did he realize, as in a hallucination, that it was no longer there. Chewing all the while, the child looked up at the old man with an angelic grin, and her eyes described a semicircle of wonder as she watched him topple backwards. His legs, rigid as the strings of a lute, formed a V above the bed. Ninna found the scene hilariously funny.

After the allotted time, Madonna Creta half-opened the door and whispered:

'Time's up, Messer Girolamo; I trust you haven't harmed the child.'

Then Madonna Creta stumbled over her client's body. Before she could steady herself, she slipped in the blood that covered the floor and fell down flat next to the dead man. Ninna, sitting in a corner, still chewing on her morsel, seemed happy with her earlier work. She smiled at Madonna Creta as if to say: 'Are you pleased? Is this how you wanted me to earn my keep?'

But that very same day, Ninna Sofia was to meet her equal.

THE WHORE-MAKER

I

ANIC-STRICKEN, MADONNA CRETA wrapped Messer Girolamo di Benedetto's corpse in a sheet, tucked the child under her arm and climbed into a small gondola. After paying in cash for the silence of the astonished gondolier, she threw overboard, into the least frequented spot of the Grand Canal, both the dead *castrato* and the child.

Fate decreed that the small and exhausted body of Ninna Sofia should wash up in the Riviera de San Benedetto, just by the dock of the Scuola that Massimo Troglio had founded thirty years earlier.

Massimo Troglio was the most prestigious *fattore delle puttane* or Whore-Maker in all of Europe. It is true that he bought, sold and even stole – much as any tradesman. But these activities were only the beginning of a long and laborious craft, the first steps in a very expensive and equally profitable business. Massimo Troglio was, above all, a teacher, a combination of filthy pedophilia and sublime pedagogical skills.

Il Fattore (as some called him) was the founder of the most

prestigious Scuola delle Puttane; the father, so to speak, of
Venice's most exquisite whores, such as Lenna Grifa herself
and the many whores who adorned the Medici court, the ones
who captured the hearts of monarchs and archbishops, the
ones in whose honor were erected the most splendid palaces of
Venice.

Not even an empress received the education lavished on the
least instructed of Massimo Troglio's ladies. The youngest,
such as Ninna Sofia, were the object of delicate care. The
madonnas (the oldest whores) were charged with looking after
them. They bathed them in she-wolf's milk, because water was
forbidden since the time of the great plagues and because,
according to Massimo Troglio, she-wolf's milk favored
growth and prevented decrepitude. They rubbed their skin
with mare's saliva to prevent the flesh from growing soft and,
once a week, they would lay their pupils down to sleep in the
barnyard, next to the pigs, to teach them to bear the most
repulsive stench and the least pleasant company.

Massimo Troglio was the author of the collection *Scuola
delle Puttane*,[7] a string of 715 aphorisms divided into seven
books, inspired no doubt by Hippocrates' *Aphorisms*.[8] Among
other things, it maintained that the best and most loyal whores
were those born from the union of '1. Carpenter and milkmaid.
2. Huntsman and Mongolian woman, or preferably a Chinese
woman. 3. Sailor and seamstress.'

---

[7] *Scuola delle Puttane* Venice, 1539.

[8] The structure of *Scuola delle Puttane* is identical to that of
Hippocrates' *Aphorisms*: it contains the same number of aphorisms per
book and its style is notably and deliberately similar.

According to Massimo Troglio, 'a woman can conceive a
child from up to seven different men whose seminal juices
blend together in the uterus and join with one another
according to the strength of each of the fathers.'

And: 'The craft of the Whore–Maker is the most sublime of
all crafts, more than that of the Perfume–Maker, more than
that of the Alchemist. Like these, we unite the vilest essences
with the most noble, the most wrathful with the kindest.'

Massimo Troglio showed himself particularly interested in
the child that Providence had bestowed upon him. So that
there should be no doubt that she was one of his novices, he
removed her bracelet and had another one made for her, of
gold and rubies, on which was written her new and definitive
name: Mona Sofia. Seldom had he seen a child of such character, of such early and abundant intelligence and, above all,
such singular and extraordinary beauty. Mona Sofia was the
synthesis of all different types of whores mingled in the body
of one child, a sort of pure and exquisite whorish extract.
And yet, Mona Sofia was not free from the two great and
mysterious threats which every Whore–Maker must face in his
wards: love and pleasure. Never had Massimo Troglio seen
such unfathomable hatred as that which the young girl
displayed toward him. Not that he was concerned by being the
object of this sentiment but, as experience had taught him,
and as Aphorism IX made clear, 'the more a woman is inclined
to hate, the more she is inclined to love.'

The second problem was not, essentially, the absence of
pain, but the suspicion that, behind her mask of insensitivity,
the more intense was Mona Sofia's pain, the more intense her
pleasure would eventually be. After all, the first stages of a

whore's education had no other immediate purpose than to teach her that both love and pleasure were forbidden emotions. The investment was too onerous and painstaking to allow the ungrateful pupil (as had happened more than once) to escape one fine day on the heels of a man with whom she might have fallen in love.

Among other aphorisms, Massimo Troglio had written:

'To corrupt is more difficult than to educate.'

'It is easier to replace one moral system with another, than to strip a person of morality.'

'Moral education is conducive to the making of whores.'

'Just like a Philosopher, a Whore-Master must be the vehicle of morality.'

'The existence of whores for money is more convenient, from the Ruler's point of view, than the existence of whores for pleasure.'

Massimo Troglio based all his theory on the Greek canon. The maxims that guided his pen and, in consequence, his practice, were, obviously, those of Aristotle's *Metaphysics*. His notion of man and woman was Aristotelian, and Aristotelian was his opinion on procreation. He lapped at the Aristotelian fount in order to explain how 'it is natural for men to make use of women's attributes'. In his chapter 'On the Monstrous Female Condition', Massimo Troglio declared: 'As Master Aristotle has said, the male sperm is the essence that transmits the characteristics of the future being. The male carries in his semen the breath, the shape, the identity, that is to say, the *kinesis* that turns an object into living matter. The male it is who gives an object its soul. Semen possesses the movement given to it by its progenitor; semen is the execution of an idea that corresponds to the shape of its progenitor, without requiring from the male the transmission of matter. In ideal circumstances, the future being will possess the complete identity of its father. The woman lends it material sustenance through its blood and its body, through the flesh that grows old and corrupt, and eventually dies. The soul's essence is always male. As the Master has taught us, the procreation of female infants is, in every case, the result of the progenitor's weakness due to sickness, old age or precocity.

'Women always supply the matter and men the creative principle: according to us, this is indeed the proper function of man and woman, and this is what it means to be male and to be female. It is necessary for the woman to provide a body and a certain amount of matter; this is not necessary for the man. Because it is not necessary for the instruments, nor for the creator, to be part of the product they fashion.'

Massimo Troglio's theory not only defines conception but also, always under the intellectual tutelage of Aristotle, it defines the very roots of every living being. 'Semen is an *organon* that possesses movement in the act.'[9] 'Semen is not a part of the growing foetus, just as no particle of the carpenter's substance passes from him to the object he is building, to become part of the wood. In the same way, no particle of semen takes part in the composition of the embryo.' And he gives this example: 'Music is not the instrument, nor is the instrument music. And yet, a piece of music corresponds exactly to the imagination of its composer.'

[9] Aristotle, *Metaphysics*, Bk VII, 9, 1034b.

The crux of Massimo Troglio's theory, as we can easily deduce, is this: the owner's rights, the *patria potestas*, the maker's rights as regards his offspring, are, in a word, the rights of the father. In the same way, it is obvious that Aristotle's purpose was simply to reaffirm the Greek rights of property.

Woman, according to this theory, was a mere adjunct whose leftover contribution to conception was the blood that flowed once a month: a mass of raw liquid, impure, unfashioned, lifeless and without shape but, of course, touched by the breath, the *kinesis*, of her weak progenitor.

This last Aristotelian revelation gave Massimo Troglio his method for the education and exploitation of women.

Mona Sofia was the most beautiful of Massimo Troglio's novices, and the one who bloomed the earliest. She also showed a premature disposition toward her profession and possessed a sensuality unusual in a girl of her age. When Mona was six, Massimo Troglio decided that the child was ready to begin the second stage of her training.

In the Scuola delle Puttane, the novices received, from a very early age, religious instruction. They were also taught ancient mythology as well as reading and writing, not only in the vernacular but also in Latin and Greek. The Scuola was, pre-eminently, a Renaissance institution, as prestigious as any of the numerous art schools. In fact, the Scuola received a subsidy from the Town Hall and each of the novices enjoyed the rank of public servant.

Mona delighted in hearing the tales told by Filipa, her teacher. Every time she heard how the whale had swallowed Jonah whole, she would open her eyes wide and beg Filipa to skip the superfluous details and tell her at once what had been the hero's fortune.

All would go well until Filipa started making accusations. Mona vehemently denied having had anything to do with the crucifixion of Our Lord Jesus Christ, and she found intolerable the assumption that He had died because of her. After all, who was she? What importance could her insignificant existence have for the fate of no less a person than the Savior Himself?

In the same vein, she declared herself innocent of all guilt and complicity in the sins of Eve whom she said she had never even met. But in the end, and much against her will, she finally assented, lowering her head without great conviction, because she was unable to stand Filipa's piercing cries, so shrill that they threatened to shatter Mona's eardrums.

 ASSIMO TROGLIO, TO HIS HONOR OR TO HIS sorrow, made Mona Sofia his most sublime creation. Ten years of teaching and care had borne fruit: she was the most beautiful woman in Venice. Her maker was patient; when his pupil was thirteen years old, he let her know that the hour of her initiation had come at last. Mona was presented in society at the *festa di presentazione* or graduation party which, every year, Massimo Troglio threw in his palazzo. It consisted of a moving ceremony during which every graduate was appointed a public functionary by one of the notables of the Republic. When Mona Sofia was announced, an awed and reverent silence overcame the assembly. Compared to the creature who had just crossed the hall's threshold, the Medici Venus was a mere peasant woman.

From all corners of Europe noble lords journeyed to the Scuola and paid out enormous fortunes. In less than six months, Massimo Troglio had recouped every last ducat invested in his pupil. During her first year, the Whore-Maker multiplied his investment by five. Mona Sofia's body had increased Massimo Troglio's wealth by two thousand gold ducats.

FREEDOM

I

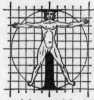T WAS DURING THE SECOND YEAR AFTER her graduation that Mona Sofia presented herself in Massimo Troglio's luxurious scriptorium. The Whore-Maker was keeping the Scuola's accounts, bent over a thick notebook with a golden spine.

'I've come to announce my freedom,' Mona Sofia declared without even an introductory greeting.

Massimo Troglio lifted his eyes from his business. He had heard the statement quite distinctly but failed to understand it, as if the speaker had been addressing him in a foreign language.

'Here is the document that frees me from your bondage,' she said, presenting him with a parchment written in red ink. 'No need to get up from your desk, simply add your signature here,' she continued, placing the parchment in front of her protector.

Massimo Troglio let out a good-natured laugh. During his long life no-one had ever asked him – if ask was the word to describe his pupil's outrageous demand – for anything so utterly shameless. He had suffered, oh yes, when several of his novices had shown themselves ungrateful enough to run away. And he had been forced to employ exemplary punishments when a runaway had been recaptured (the usual corrective measure entailed lopping off a toe). But for a novice to burst into his own office with such unheard-of demands was, quite simply, madness.

'May I remind you that the Scuola has its statutes and rules,' Massimo Troglio began to say, beaming a warm and paternal smile, 'therefore . . .'

Before her Master was able to finish his sentence, Mona Sofia pulled out a golden-handled knife and pressed the tip against her breast. With complete self-assurance she said:

'My body has more than paid you back for the education you bestowed upon me and, if you care to hear me say so, let me tell you how grateful I am and let me offer you both reverence and respect. But now I demand that you grant me what is mine: my own body.'

Massimo Troglio grew white in the face and then flushed red with anger. Trying to remain calm, he spoke:

'You are of no use to me dead. I can, if you wish, sign as you demand but what makes you think I will not bring you back under the rights granted to me by law? And you know very well what my punishment consists of.'

Mona Sofia smiled.

'You wouldn't dare damage a hair on my body. I am your creation. But don't think I'm ungrateful. If you read the parchment, you will see that I've not forgotten you. I'll give you a tenth of all the money I earn with my body until the day one of us dies. Your option is the tenth part of my earnings, or nothing at all,' she said, pressing the knife upon her breast so that a drop of blood rolled down onto her belly.

Massimo Troglio dipped the pen in the inkwell and signed the parchment. Mona Sofia knelt by his feet and kissed her master's hands. Then she left the Scuola for ever.

Alone in his scriptorium, Massimo Troglio wept inconsolably. He wept like a child.

He wept like a father.

HOW MATEO COLOMBO MET
MONA SOFIA

I

T WAS DURING HIS BRIEF SOJOURN IN Venice, in the fall of 1557, that the anatomist met Mona Sofia. It was in the palace of a certain duke, on the occasion of a ball organized by the host himself for his birthday. Mona Sofia was by then an experienced grown-up woman. She was fifteen years old.

Perhaps because Leonardo da Vinci had declared his puzzlement as to why men were ashamed of their virility and 'hid their sexual organs when they ought solemnly to decorate them, as they would a high-ranking minister', that year it had become the custom among fashionable men to exhibit and gaudily festoon their genitals. Almost all the guests, except the very elderly, wore light-colored tights that showed off their owners' private parts with ribbons tied to the waist and groin. Those who had larger reasons to be grateful to their Creator, embraced the new fashion wholeheartedly. Those who did not, employed various methods to adapt to the times without needing to feel ashamed. In the Bottega del Moro, prosthetic devices were sold for placing under the clothes to lend fortune to those less fortunate. Among the many adornments, from diadems in precious stones that ringed the 'minister' to showy nettings of stringed pearls, were ribbons tied to four or five bells that betrayed with their tinkles the moods of 'his lordship'. According to the tinkling of the bells, the ladies were able to measure their acceptance among the men.

It was a ball like any other, and began with the kissing-dance whose rules or steps were dictated by each participant's mood. The name derived from the fact that when the couples came together or parted again, they were obliged to do so with a kiss.

Mateo Colombo stood apart from the dancers and, although he was not an old man, he wore the traditional *lucco* which, among so much display of masculine thighs, gave him an imposing appearance. As a result, he saw himself rewarded with more female glances than those who displayed their majestic belfries, real or fake.

Not halfway through the ball, Mona Sofia made her entrance. She did not need to have herself announced. At the door, two Moorish slaves helped her down from her palanquin. Until then, two or three of the women present had held most of the attention; now, the most beautiful among them felt malformed, lame or hunchbacked, compared to the new arrival. Mona Sofia towered to an august height. She wore a dress split from the bottom to the top of her legs. The translucent silk revealed her body to perfection. At every step, her breasts quivered along her neckline, showing the upper moon of her nipples. From her forehead dangled an emerald whose purpose was merely to be outshone by the brilliance of her eyes.

Mona Sofia was greeted by a veritable carillon, the sound of hundreds of masculine bells.

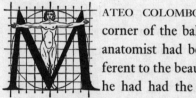ATEO COLOMBO STOOD IN A SOLITARY corner of the ballroom. Like the others, the anatomist had been unable to remain indifferent to the beauty of the newcomer. In fact, he had had the impertinence to turn away from a hypochondriac lady who wouldn't stop listing her infirmities, and had left her talking to herself.

Mona Sofia was welcomed by the host who made her join at once the kissing-dance. It was customary that a gentleman would invite a lady with a kiss and then, after a few turns, the lady would replace her partner with another, and so on until the end. Of course, the dance lent itself to a game of seduction. The convention was as follows: if a lady failed to be interested in any of the gentlemen, then her way out of the bind was to invite a married man; if a lady chose a single man, her intentions were clear. There were also conventions surrounding the kiss. If a lady barely brushed a gentleman's cheek, then she meant nothing but to dance and enjoy herself; a loud and affectionate kiss indicated less formal intentions, such as marriage.

But if the kiss landed on the gentleman's lips, then the lascivious purposes of the lady were clear: it was an obvious and outright invitation to sex.

Mona Sofia was dancing in a manner that one might call Oriental, both hands on her waist while swaying her hips. Everyone was waiting with curious impatience for the moment she would be forced to choose a new partner; this was why all the young men were fighting to take the front row, showing off, with deliberate obscenity, their voluminous and decorated members. But Mona Sofia had already known many of these gentlemen who were now displaying unexplained virilities, when they had stood unadorned except for their birthrights. She would glance at each of the men waiting to be chosen, would approach them and then, when she seemed on the point of making up her mind, she would turn on her heels and dance toward another man whom she would also, eventually, dismiss. Still dancing to the sound of the lutes, Mona Sofia made her way through the throng of enthusiastic gallants. And Mateo Colombo suddenly noticed that Mona's breasts, trembling along the rim of her neckline, were pointing their nipples at him. Mona Sofia was advancing with apparent determination toward the anatomist.

Under other circumstances, Mateo Colombo would have felt embarrassed. But now, seeing a woman coming toward him, a woman who was staring at him in a manner he had never experienced before, he was unable to shake off the impression that there was no-one else in the room. And yet, he could hear the bustle of the dancers and the music of the lutes; he could even see the crowds of guests. He felt exactly like a mouse facing a snake. Even had he wanted to, he was unable to see anything except the green eyes that outshone the supercilious emerald. Mona Sofia brought her lips close to those of the anatomist (he could inhale her breath of mint and rosewater) and at the edge of his mouth he felt, like a warm, quick breeze, the brief touch of Mona Sofia's tongue. He danced, oh yes. He never lost his composure, certainly not. He behaved with utmost courtesy. He was even able to conceal the fact that, from that day forward until the day of his death, he felt a vital need for that mint-and-rosewater-scented breath, that warm breeze, those green eyes. He danced. No-one could have known that, like someone bitten by a serpent, the dancing man was mortally ill. He simply danced.

For ever more, until his dying day, he would remember dancing under the charm of those malicious eyes. As if commemorating the date of his martyrdom, he would remember the flight down passageways, gardens and galleries, and how, in a hidden room of the palazzo, to the faraway plucking of the lutes, he had kissed her pink nipples, hard as pearls but smooth as petals. Until his dying day he would remember, as a somber and yet sweet anniversary, her voice like crackling wood and the scandal of her tongue made of the fire of Hell. He'd remember how, like a famished man postponing his first meal in order to delay the enjoyment, he rejected her body and, settling his *lucco*, said to her:

'I want to paint your portrait.'

And like a shipwrecked sailor mistaking the clouds on the horizon for land, he imagined he saw signs of love in the green and heavily lashed eyes.

'I want to paint your portrait,' he said again, with emotion.

And he imagined seeing the same emotion in the serpent's

eyes. Mona Sofia kissed him with great tenderness.

'You can come and see me whenever you like,' she said, and added in a whisper:

'Come tomorrow.'

The anatomist watched her straighten her dress, offer him one last time her nipples to be kissed, and turn toward the door. Then he heard her say, before disappearing:

'Come tomorrow, I'll be waiting.'

The land was nothing but clouds.

III

HE NEXT DAY, AT PRECISELY FIVE O'CLOCK in the afternoon, Mateo Colombo climbed the seven steps up to the Bordello del Fauno Rosso. He was carrying his portable easel folded on his back, the canvas held against his chest, the palette under his right arm and the bagful of oil paints hanging from the belt of his *lucco*. He was in fact so laden that he almost collided with the brothelkeeper.

As Mateo Colombo peered through the open door, Mona Sofia, covered in a transparent veil, had just finished plaiting her hair in front of her vanity mirror. The anatomist, standing at the threshold with his burden of equipment, saw reflected in the mirror the eyes which yesterday had seemed to him so full of love. And here they were now, for him alone, for his eyes only. He cleared his throat to announce his presence.

Without turning, without even glancing up, Mona Sofia beckoned him in.

'I've come to do your portrait,' he said.

Still without turning, Mona Sofia merely answered:

'Whatever you do during your visit is indifferent to me.' And immediately added: 'In case you don't know, the fee is ten ducats.'

'Do you remember me?' Mateo Colombo murmured.

'If I could see your face . . .' she said to her anonymous visitor hidden behind his canvas.

The anatomist put down his load and Mona Sofia inspected him in her mirror.

'I don't think I've met you before,' she said doubtfully. Once again she reminded him of the fee: 'Ten ducats.'

Mateo Colombo left the ten ducats on the bedside table, set up the canvas on the easel, pulled out the oils from his bag, laid out his brushes and, without saying a word, began the portrait he would call *Woman in Love*.

IV

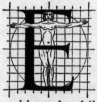VERY DAY, WHEN THE AUTOMATA IN THE clock tower sounded the fifth stroke, Mateo Colombo would climb the seven steps up to the brothel on Via Bocciari, enter Mona's room, leave the ten ducats on the bedside table and, while setting up the canvas, without even taking off his coat, he would tell Mona that he loved her and that, even though she refused to acknowledge it, he could see the love in her eyes. Between brushstrokes he would beg her to leave the brothel and go with him across Monte Veldo, to Padua; tell her that, if she so wished, he was ready to give up his classroom at the university. And Mona, lying naked on the bed, her nipples hard as almonds and smooth as petals, kept staring at the clock tower outside the window, waiting for the bells to strike again. And when they finally did, she would look up at her visitor with eyes full of malice.

'Your time is up,' she would say, and go to her dresser.

And every day, at five o'clock in the afternoon, when the shadows of the columns of St Theodore and the winged lion joined to create a single slanted line across the Piazza di San Marco, the anatomist would arrive at the brothel with his canvas, easel and paints, leave the ten ducats on her table and never take off his *lucco*. Mixing the colors on his palette, he would tell her that he loved her, and that, even if she refused to see it, he himself could tell when love settled in someone's eyes. He would tell her that not even the hand of a god was able to reproduce such beauty, and that, if the brothelkeeper were to disapprove of their wedding, he was willing to pay for her all the money he had, entreating her to leave the awful brothel and come with him to his family home in Cremona. And Mona Sofia, without even seeming to listen, would caress her smooth thighs, firm as if carved in wood, waiting for the first of the six bells to signal that her client's time was up.

And every day, at exactly five o'clock in the afternoon, when the waters in the canal would begin to climb the steps to the landing, Mateo Colombo would arrive at the brothel on Via Bocciari, close to the Church of the Holy Trinity, and, without taking the *beretta* off his head, would leave the ten ducats on the bedside table. While setting up the canvas on the easel, he would tell her that he loved her, that they should run away together across Monte Veldo or, if necessary, across the Mediterranean Sea. And Mona, locked in her cynical silence, would maliciously tuck her plait beneath her body, caress her nipples and pay no attention to the progress of the portrait. She would look at nothing but the clock tower, waiting for the bell to strike which would enable her to say the only words she seemed capable of uttering:

'Your time is up.'

And every day, at five o'clock in the afternoon, when the sun was a warm glimmer multiplied tenfold over the roofs of St Mark, the anatomist, laden with bags and dangling equipment, would humbly leave ten ducats on the table and, in the midst of the scent of oil paints and other men's sex, would tell her that he loved her, that he was willing to give up all that was his and buy her back, and run away with her to the far coast of the Mediterranean or, if necessary, to the New World beyond the Atlantic Ocean. And Mona, without saying a word, would caress the parrot slumbering on her shoulder, as if there were no-one else in the room, waiting for the automata in the clock tower to move once again. And then, with eyes full of sensual malice, she would say:

'Your time is up.'

And during his entire stay in Venice, every day at exactly five o'clock in the afternoon, the anatomist would visit the brothel on Via Bocciari close to the Holy Trinity, and tell her he loved her. And so it was until the anatomist came to the end of his painting and his money. His time in Venice was up.

Humiliated, destitute, broken-hearted and alone except for his crow, Mateo Colombo returned to Padua with a single purpose in mind.

THE SPICE ROUTE

I

FTER HIS RETURN TO PADUA, MATEO
Colombo spent most of his time ensconced in
his cell. He would barely leave to attend the
obligatory Masses and teach in the anatomy
theatre. His furtive visits to the morgue
became infrequent and, in the end, he abandoned them
entirely. He stopped showing interest in cadavers. Locked in
his cell, he did little more than hunt through ancient pharma-
cological volumes which he once had used to study. When he
ventured into the woods close to the abbey, he seemed no
longer curious about the remains Leonardino would discover
for him. Suddenly, the anatomist had become a harmless
herbivore, a mere pharmacologist. He would fill bags with all
sorts of herbs which he would carefully classify, store and later
brew.

He studied the properties of mandragora and belladonna, of
hemlock and wild celery, and noted the effects of these plants
on the different human organs. His task was dangerous,
because the boundaries that separated pharmacology from

witchcraft were vague and ill-defined. Belladonna had long interested both doctors and wizards. The ancient Greeks had called it *atropa*, 'the inflexible one', and attributed to it the gift of cutting or restoring the thread of life. Italians knew the plant well and the ladies of Florence would apply its sap to dilate their pupils and bestow a daydreamer's look which would lend them an incomparable charm, at the cost of more or less chronic blindness. And the anatomist knew of the hallucinogenic effects of the fearful black henbane whose properties had been described in the Egyptian papyrus of Eber, twenty-five hundred years before, and it is certain he knew that Albert the Great had written how sorcerers used henbane to conjure up demons from Hell.

He prepared hundreds of potions whose formulas were punctiliously cataloged and, during the night, he visited the sordid brothels of Padua laden with his bottles. Mateo Colombo had set himself a long-sought-for goal: to obtain a potion that would control the capricious will of women. Of course, there existed numerous love-potions that every witch's apprentice would prepare for a handful of ducats. But the anatomist still preserved a measure of sanity which prevented him from being taken in by such quackeries. After all, he was a graduate in pharmacology and he knew full well the properties of plants. He had read Paracelsus, and the ancient Greek doctors, and the Arab herbalists.

Among his notes is the following:

In order to insure that a potion is effective, it must be ingested through the mouth and from there into the digestive system. Applications on the skin may also yield results, but this method is more laborious and its fruits weaker and more ephemerous. It can also be delivered contra natura, *through the anal orifice, but under such circumstances it is difficult for the body to retain it, resulting in serious attacks of diarrhea. In certain cases, it may be possible to inhale the potion in the form of vapors and thereby distribute its particles through the lungs into the blood. But the recommended path is undoubtedly through the mouth.*

But how was he to get the whores to drink his potions willingly? The most practical method was to rub his penis with the brews, highly concentrated, and via fellatio let them find their way into the women's bodies.

The effects were dreadful.

On the first occasion, Mateo Colombo tried an infusion of belladonna and mandragora in equal proportions. His victim was a stout and elderly *mamma*, an old whore from the brothel situated on the top floor of the Taverna del Mulo, an ancient strumpet by the name of Laverda. He paid half a florin for her, which was certainly too high a price. However, he paid without arguing.

Before swallowing her client's morsel, Laverda gargled with a sip of rancid wine which, since it had been blessed, had the property of guarding from contagious diseases and demonic possessions. The anatomist knew that this custom had its roots in superstition and did not think it would affect the success of his experiment. Laverda was a woman knowledgeable in the art of fellatio, a skill favored by the fact that she lacked every last tooth, so that her client's member could slide in with ease, undisturbed. The anatomist noticed immediately the first signs of the potion's effect: Laverda stopped her work, stood up and stared at the anatomist with exultant eyes and a sudden excitement that brought color to her old cheeks. Mateo Colombo felt his heart jump.

'I think I'm—', Laverda started to say. 'I think I'm—'

'In love?'

'—poisoned,' she completed and immediately vomited every last drop in her guts onto the *lucco* of her client.

After this unfortunate incident, Mateo Colombo prepared an infusion with the same herbs but in unequal proportions. If the first potion had provoked boundless loathing, then, logically, changing the proportions would provoke the contrary effect. He felt he was on the right path.

The following week he climbed, once again, the stairs that led to the brothel. He had smeared himself with the new potion but the results were no less disastrous. His second victim was Calandra, a young whore who had only recently started her career. After suffering a fainting spell, she awoke; in horror, she saw all manner of devils fluttering through the room and landing at the anatomist's feet. The hideous visions gradually disappeared and left in their place a stubborn mystical delirium.

Mateo Colombo decided it might be best to replace the belladonna with henbane. And so he did.

HEN MATEO COLOMBO ENTERED THE tavern, he was greeted by a deadly silence. The customers closest to the door edged their way toward the entrance and, once in the street, took to their heels as if in fear of their lives. As the anatomist advanced toward the back of the tavern, the rest of the customers retreated to both sides, greeting him with a mixture of reverence and awe. He climbed the stairs and, from the top, looked back to see that in the time it had taken him to reach the landing, the tavern had completely emptied. Even the old innkeeper was nowhere to be seen.

He was so astonished, he couldn't even guess the cause of the customers' terror. He knocked at the small door of the brothel but could make out no sounds on the other side. He was about to turn away when he noticed that the door was unlocked. He did not mean to enter uninvited, but he felt that the crack between the door and its frame was an invitation of sorts. The hinges creaked inhospitably and Mateo Colombo stepped in. At the back of the room he could see a figure standing in the gloomy flicker from the light of a three-branched candlestick.

'I was waiting for you,' said the figure, in a warm feminine voice. 'Come closer.'

Mateo Colombo advanced a few steps and then recognized Beatrice, the youngest of the novices, a child who had not yet reached her twelfth birthday.

'I know you well, come closer,' Beatrice repeated, extending her hand. 'I knew you would come. There is no need to deceive me, not me. I know the time of the Great Prophecy has come. Before possessing me, know that both my body and my soul are yours.'

The anatomist looked over his shoulder to make sure she wasn't speaking to somebody else.

'I know what you did to Laverda and Calandra.'

The anatomist blushed and made a silent prayer for the health of the two innocent women.

'Make me completely yours,' Beatrice said in a throaty voice and let out a wicked laugh.

'That is why I've come . . .' Mateo Colombo hesitated before pulling out two ducats from his moneybag.

But Beatrice didn't even glance at the money.

'You don't know how long I've loved you in silence. You don't know how long I've waited for you.'

'You were waiting for me?'

'I knew today was the day. There is the full moon preying on Jupiter,' Beatrice said, pointing to the night sky outside the window. 'Don't you realize I'm familiar with the prophecies of the astrologer Giorgio de Novara? I know that he said that the conjunction of Jupiter with Saturn gave birth to the Laws of Moses; with Mars, to the Chaldean religion; with the sun to the Egyptian faith; with Venus to the appearance of Mohammed and with Mercury, to Jesus Christ.' She paused and, staring straight into his eyes, pointed at the anatomist:

'Today is the conjunction of Jupiter and the moon.'

Mateo Colombo looked out of the window and saw the full, luminous moon. Then he turned inquiringly to Beatrice.

'Today!' she answered in a strangled cry. 'Today is the day of your Return! The Age of the Antichrist has come! I belong to you! Make me yours!' she said, pulling away the blanket that was covering her beautiful and naked body.

Mateo Colombo was slow in understanding.

'May the power of God be with me,' he whispered, made the sign of the Cross, and then burst out in sudden anger:

'You fool! You idiot girl! Do you want to see me burnt at the stake?'

He lifted his hand and was about to strike the possessed child when he suddenly realized that he had become a dangerous being. To be accused of diabolical activities was a serious matter, but much more serious was to have incited involuntary allegiances to the Devil. He could see himself fleeing Padua, pursued by a host of demonic followers.

Before Beatrice's story had time to spread like seeds in the wind, and while waiting for the situation in Padua to quiet down, the anatomist decided to request a commission in Venice. And to justify the journey to himself, and not lose sight of his guiding purpose, he clung to Paracelsus' words:

'How can someone cure Germany's diseases with medi-
cines that God placed far away, on the banks of the Nile?'[10]
This was the phrase that would lead him on the wildest of
pilgrimages.

[10] Paracelsus, *Writings*.

III

E TRAVELED TO VENICE. HE COLLECTED
and labeled the herbs that grew in the
countryside, the moss left by the nightly tides
at the foot of the landing steps, and even the
fetid mushrooms growing in the manure
collected in the palatial aqueducts. He was on the point of
preparing his potion when he heard that, as a child, Mona Sofia
had been bought in Greece. Before leaving for the Aegean, he
punished his wounded spirit by furtively watching Mona's
progress about the Piazza di San Marco. Hidden behind the
cathedral's columns, he watched her, in all her arrogant
beauty, carried in her palanquin by her two Moorish slaves,
preceded by the Dalmatian bitch as her guard of honor. He
mortified himself by observing her sculpted legs, her nipples
trembling at the edge of her neckline to the rhythm of her black
servants' step. He tortured himself by staring at the green eyes
that tarnished the emerald dangling from her brow.

HERBS OF THE GODS

I

N THE NECKLACE OF ISLANDS THAT surround the peninsula, Mateo Colombo collected his plants and used their sap to prepare his brews. In Thessaly he picked henbane, under whose narcotic influence the ancient priestesses of Delphi uttered their prophecies; in Boetia, fresh leaves of the deadly nightshade; in Argos, he dug up the mandrake root, whose sinister anthropomorphism was described by Pythagoras, taking good care to cover his ears because, as its collectors knew well, if the root is extracted without skill and precaution, the plant's agonizing cries may drive a man to madness; in Crete he gathered the seeds of *dutura metel*, mentioned in ancient Chinese and Sanskrit manuscripts, whose properties were described by Avicenna in the eleventh century; in Khios, the fearful *dutura ferox*, an aphrodisiac so powerful that, according to the ancient chronicles, it could make the penis burst, and the patient bleed to death. And he made sure that each and every one of his herbs, roots and seeds was a good and healthy specimen.

II

N ATHENS, ON THE SLOPES OF THE HILL OF the Acropolis, Mateo Colombo learned what was 'Good, Beautiful and True'. Drunk with the Hellenic past and a previously undiscovered paganism, and also with a certain cannabis described by Galen, mixed with belladonna, he realized the misery of life in the Renaissance. He now found himself in the golden cradle of true Antiquity and here he opened his bag of divine herbs and made sure that they were wholesome. He took a bite of the *amarita muscaria*, and saw the Beginning of All Things. He saw Eurynome rise from the darkness of Chaos, he saw her move through the Dance of Creation separating the seas from the heavens and giving birth to the Winds. And he, the anatomist, became Pelasgus, the first man, whom Eurynome taught to feed himself. The Goddess of All Things offered him, in the palm of her hand, the red seed of the *claviceps purpurea*, and as he ate it he became the first of Chronos's sons.

Lying on his back on the slopes of the hill of the Acropolis, he said to himself that this, indeed, was living, and that death was nothing but a horrible dream. He lit a small bonfire and burnt a few belladonna leaves and then inhaled the smoke. By his side, he now saw the Maenads in the Dionysian orgies, and he could lay his hands on them, feel their burning looks, and see how they stretched out their arms to embrace him. He was now in the bowels of Antiquity, at the Gates of Eleusis, celebrating and thanking the gods for their gift of earthly seeds.

There was no need to dig in the millenary mud, no need to rummage in archives or libraries. There, in front of his eyes, was Hellenic Antiquity. In his lungs was the air breathed by Solon and Pisistratus. Everything lay on the surface, in broad daylight. It wasn't necessary to translate manuscripts or decipher ruins. Any of the peasants walking along the horizon were cut by the hand of Phidias, and the eyes of any simpleton had the same fire as those of the Seven Sages of Greece. What was Venice, what was Florence but a coarse and pretentious imitation? What was Botticelli's *Primavera* compared to the landscape offered to him at the foot of the hill of the Acropolis? What were the Milanese Visconti or the Bolognese Bentivoglios, what the Mantuan Gonzagas or the Perugian Baglioni, what the Sforzas of Pesaro or the Medici themselves, compared to the poorest laborer of Athens? All these new lords had no more lineage or nobility than their coats of arms, granted to them by their insolent *condottieri*. The neediest beggar of Piraeus carried in his veins the noble blood of Clisthenes. What was the great Lorenzo de' Medici compared to Pericles? All these questions crossed his mind when there, on the slopes of the hill of the Acropolis, he fell soundly and peacefully asleep.

OAKED IN ICE–COLD DEW, MATEO COLOMBO awoke the following morning. Next to him were the remains of a small fire. He tried to stand up but he lost his balance and rolled down the hill. His head ached horribly. But he remembered perfectly the events of the previous day. In fact, his memories were clearer than the landscape which now, hazy and unfocused, offered itself to his eyes: merely a bare field sprinkled with inhospitable rocks. This was his much–desired 'Antiquity'. He felt ashamed; he hastily made the sign of the Cross, and begged the One and All-Powerful God to forgive him for his unaccountable infatuation with paganism. He vomited.

But he hadn't forgotten the reason for his voyage. In the port of Piraeus he collected anything of a vegetable nature growing among the bricks of the brothel and tavern walls behind which, between drinks, the pimps conducted their trade.

He was ready to mix precise proportions of herbs, roots,

seeds and mushrooms, when he heard, from the lips of the very man who had bought her, that Mona Sofia had been born in Corsica. Therefore, following Paracelsus' dictum, he traveled to the Island of the Pirates.

ATEO COLOMBO TRAVELED WITH THE DE-
votion of a penitent on the road to the Holy
Land. He followed Mona Sofia's footsteps
with the mystical adoration of a man on the Via
Crucis and, as he advanced, his veneration and
martyrdom grew accordingly. He hoped to find the key to the
Revelation of the Mystery which seemed to him, with every
step, more and more distant. And as he journeyed backwards,
toward the murky seas of Gorgar the Black, he might have
written as his Genoese namesake had done to his faraway
queen:

*During many days of fearful storm I never saw the sun nor the
stars above the sea: the ships had gashes in them, the sails were
torn, anchors and riggings and supplies were lost. The crew
were sick. Contrite, many promising to enter the religious life,
my mariners would make confession to one another. Their pain
tore at my soul. Pity tore at my heart. I am exceedingly weary
and my infirmity opens once again my wounds. I have little*

hope of life. Men's eyes never saw a sea so high, so ugly, made
of foam. A sea of blood, boiling as in a cauldron lit by a great
fire. Never were the heavens so awe-inspiring.

And Mateo Colombo, equally despairing, traveled on board
a ship that was as fragile as a nut-shell and often in danger of
crashing against the rocks. Nor was he allowed to reach the
Corsican shore: the pirates of Gorgar the Black attacked
the ship, robbed it of its cargo, murdered its crew and many
of the passengers, and only by a miracle was the anatomist's
life saved. During the attack, Gorgar was wounded in a lung;
Mateo Colombo healed his wound and, out of gratitude, the
pirate gave him his freedom.

His spirit still unsettled by the potent Greek herbs, his body
sick with cold and damp, his soul in pieces, Mateo Colombo
returned to Padua.

Like a spice-seeker stumbling upon a splendid gold mine,
or like his Genoese namesake, Mateo Colombo was destined
to discover his America. Chance was to reveal to him that
by traveling west he could reach the east. Fate would show
him that, in order to arrive victorious in Venice, he would first
have to roam through Florence, and that before ruling over the
heart of one woman, he would first have to conquer the heart
of another.

And so it was.

PART TWO

INÉS DE TORREMOLINOS

I

ACK IN PADUA, TWO ITEMS OF NEWS awaited him, one good, the other bad. The bad news came from the dean.

'Much is said about you in Padua,' Alessandro di Legnano began. 'And certainly nothing praiseworthy.'

The dean told the anatomist that Beatrice, the novice at the brothel of the Taverna del Mulo, had been put on trial and burnt for witchcraft.

'She mentioned you in her deposition,' he said laconically.

Mateo Colombo remained silent.

'If it were up to me,' the dean continued, 'I'd haul you in front of the Inquisition this very day.' He watched the anatomist grow pale. 'And yet, luck seems to be on your side.'

He then proceeded to tell him that a certain abbot, a relation of the Medici, had summoned the anatomist to Florence. A Castilian lady, the widow of a Florentine nobleman, the Marquis of Malagamba, was on her death bed and the anatomist's services were required. A thousand florins had been paid in advance and another five hundred were available should he require the help of an apprentice. The dean considered it a fair proposition: to put aside the matter of Beatrice and the depositions of her fellow whores, Laverda and Calandra, in exchange for the fee offered for the skills of his subordinate.

'You will leave for Florence tomorrow,' Alessandro di Legnano concluded. And before dismissing Mateo Colombo, he added: 'As far as an apprentice is concerned, Bertino will be traveling with you. The decision is final.'

To argue would have been useless. Mateo Colombo nodded his agreement; the dean had left him no margin to negotiate. Bertino's proper name was Alberto and he carried the dean's surname. No-one knew exactly what their relationship was, but Bertino was known to be the dean's eyes and ears. Even more foolish than his protector, Bertino would become the anatomist's shadow during his sojourn in Florence.

NÉS WAS THE ELDEST OF THE DAUGHTERS of Don Rodrigo Torremolinos, Count of Urquijo and Lord of Navarra, and of Isabel de Alba, Duchess of Cuernavaca and Countess of Urquijo. To her father's eternal regret, the couple had no male offspring. Therefore, being the firstborn female, her little highness enjoyed the rights of *potestas* and *divitia*. Such rank and lineage, however, were in marked contrast to the poor health resulting from her premature birth, which lent her a pale frailty and a sickly and diminutive figure. As if the small body were not big enough to house a soul, as a baby she had looked half dead: not as if she were about to give up the ghost, but as if the ghost had never taken up residence inside her. The cradle with its leafy canopy, built for her by the best carpenter in Castile, was so vast that the tiny Inés seemed invisible among the folds of silk. The only evidence of life was her rattling breath that always seemed to be her last. The carpenter, after finishing the cradle, had begun to build a small coffin. As the days went by, the child lost even

more weight, if what appeared like mere absence could have any weight at all. The wet-nurse, seeing that little Inés lacked the strength even to grip her teat, had given up all hope, and it seemed as if the infant was going to receive the last sacrament before ever receiving the first. However, God knows how, little Inés survived. Gradually, like buds on a dry branch, the color of life appeared on the girl's cheeks. And as the child grew, in inverse proportion, the family fortune started to diminish. The olive groves and vineyards of the noble household, once the most splendid and generous in the peninsula, and whose abundance was documented on the family's coat of arms, were devastated by a sudden plague that, from one day to the next, gobbled up anything with the slightest shade of green. Don Rodrigo, a ruined man, with no other fortune than his sorrow and his titles, cursed his wife's womb which, like a sick land that breeds nothing but useless weeds, had been incapable of fashioning a male of his blood who might, at the very least, have brought a dowry into the household coffers. But it became evident that the Duchess could only give birth to feeble girls. In despair, Don Rodrigo traveled to Florence to ask his cousin, the Marquis of Malagamba, for help. The Spanish nobleman begged, prayed and even wept. The Marquis, who shared not only his cousin's blood but also the business of keeping olive groves, was a compassionate and charitable gentleman. He offered his cousin a fortune in words of encouragement and faith, but as for money, not a single florin. Don Rodrigo returned to Castile forlorn. However, the very next summer a messenger came, bringing a letter from the Marquis. To the Count's amazement, he read that his kinsman requested his daughter Inés's hand in marriage and,

in exchange, was offering the sum of money Don Rodrigo had
begged for the previous winter. The proposal had a reason: the
Marquis was a childless widower. He needed a means of
obtaining a legitimate son – that is to say, he needed a wife.
Furthermore, his union with a Castilian family would be
beneficial, since it would allow him to extend his domains as
far as the Iberian peninsula. The messenger returned to
Florence with Don Rodrigo's consent. Inés, at the time, was
thirteen years old.

There was to be no courtship and no seduction, no love
letters and no gifts, except the gift of Inés herself sent by her
parents to Florence, where her husband was awaiting her,
accompanied by a *corps-de-garde* made up of members from
both households. Inés was married in a virtuous and virginal
state. The Marquis was of the noble race of Charlemagne, and
the impression Inés first had of her husband was that he
carried about his person the collective girth of all his illustrious
ancestors and the sum of years of all the celebrated Carolingian
generations. She never thought of her husband as being old
and fat, but neither did she see him as young and slender.

Inés was a good wife who displayed toward her husband a
proper *virtus in conjugio*. She knew how to show her fine
breeding and her chaste Christian devotion in marriage. If a
wife, according to the apostolic precept, should forgo all
passion and 'use her husband as if she didn't have one', Inés
never found the task at all difficult. In fact, she barely fitted in
the bed next to her incommensurable spouse. She had no need
to control rapturous passion. She felt no attraction toward her
husband nor, indeed, toward any man. It could be said that
Inés had no inclination toward sensuality. Nothing gave her

pleasure or provoked her disgust. She knew nothing of cries and murmurs, nor of nightly impulses. During the entire course of her marriage, the Marquis had three senile erections; three times they knew one another and three times she gave birth without ever understanding what was meant by *frenesi veneris*. As if a curse had fallen on the family, just like her mother Inés had no sons, only daughters, dead wood on the ancient Carolingian family tree. A fourth erection would have been a miracle; therefore the Marquis, weary, indignant and forlorn, decided to give up trying and simply die. And so he did.

III

NÉS WAS VERY YOUNG. SHE GAVE HERSELF over entirely to bringing up her three mishaps, somewhat saddened by the memory of her husband, whose wish for continuity she hadn't been able to fulfill. She put all her spirit into works of charity, compassion, benevolence and, above everything else, into God. In the privacy of her room, she wrote innumerable poems in His praise. She prayed. She was one of the richest women in all of Florence.

She carried her widowhood with no other sorrow than that of not having been able to fulfill the sanctity of marriage, as proved by the glory of a male heir. Otherwise, she needed no other love than that of God. She didn't feel deprived of a man's consoling company; she felt no longing for sweet conjugal pleasures nor was she ever invaded by dark and sinful thoughts because, to tell the truth, she never knew the former and she was unable to imagine the latter.

Yet all the wealth Inés had inherited was not enough to staunch the pain of having been incapable of giving her late husband a male child. Therefore, to alleviate her sorrow and, above all, to expiate her fault in memory of her spouse, she decided to sell the olive groves, the vineyards and the castles, and with the money build an abbey. In this manner, through a chaste and celibate life, she would fulfill the responsibilities of matrimony, becoming a servant of the sons her womb had not known how to bring forth: the monastic brotherhood and the poor. And so she did.

It was said that Inés was on the path toward sanctity until – it is proper to mention it now – a man came to stand between her unblemished life and her eternal glory: Mateo Renaldo Colombo.

IV

NÉS WAS CLOSE TO ENDING HER DAYS AS A true saint. In the summer of 1558, her health suffered from an unknown sickness and, though still very young, she retired with her three daughters to humble lodgings close to the abbey she had established, where she decided to await premature death with Christian forbearance.

Inés's spirit had gradually turned gloomy and pessimistic, and she withdrew into a dark and troubled world. Any event in the slightest unusual, or even something trivial and ordinary, was in her eyes a sign of black foreboding. If the bells of the abbey rang for whatever reason, she believed they were ringing because one of her daughters was dead. She was concerned about the abbot's health, which was excellent, and indeed about that of anyone around her. The slightest cold announced a fatal bout of pneumonia. In time, all these fears were directed toward herself and she began to suspect that she suffered from the most terrible diseases. A simple skin irritation became a symptom of incipient leprosy. She felt haunted by death. She suffered from chronic insomnia during which her heart seemed to leap out of her chest, and from a painful shortness of breath that made her certain she would die suffocated. She would be seized by sudden cold sweats. In the solitary confinement of her bed, she would imagine what her young body would look like after death and she was tormented by the idea of her decomposing flesh. Eventually, this distressing malaise spread beyond her bedtime and took over her life completely. Frightened by the vertigo that threatened to loosen the ground beneath her feet, Inés decided to take definitive refuge in her bed and await the will of God. But not even in God did she find peace or comfort, and this added to her torment; in spite of her piety she was unable to await her death with Christian forbearance. Inés had all the appearance of a soul in agony.

Seeing that Inés's health was undoubtedly failing, the abbot recalled that in Padua a surgeon had miraculously saved the life of a dying man, an event that had provoked much comment at the time. Therefore, without hesitation, he interceded with an illustrious cousin close to the Medici, who, without giving the expense a second thought, sent him a thousand florins to pay for the doctor's fees and another five hundred for the journey and for whatever unforeseen costs might arise.

THE DISCOVERY

I

 RIDER FLEW AT FULL SPEED THROUGH THE narrow lanes of Padua. In his haste, he upset a stall in the Piazza dei Frutti, giving the stall-holder no time even to shout back a curse, and leaving a trail of oranges rolling down the street. His horse was dripping with sweat and foaming at the mouth; it had come at a gallop from the other side of the Euganean Mountains. Leonardino, the crow, saw him coming and watched furtively. Flying in circles, he saw the rider cross the ancient walls through the Porta Euganea and then, further on, course down the Riviera de San Benedetto. When he crossed the Ponte Tadi over the canal, the crow flew ahead and, as if knowing in advance the rider's destination, he perched over the door to the room where his master used to lecture.

The rider dismounted at the gates of the university and ran across the courtyard.

'Where can I find Mateo Colombo?' he asked a man he had practically knocked down.

The man happened to be the dean, Alessandro di Legnano.

The messenger briefly explained the urgency of his business, but without giving more details than those which a formal courtesy required, and asked once again for Mateo Colombo, making it clear that he had instructions not to state his business to anyone other than the anatomist himself.

'I'm to deliver a message to Messer Mateo Renaldo Colombo in person,' the messenger explained laconically.

The dean was profoundly irritated by the respectful manner in which the messenger spoke of the *barbiere* but, even more, by the way this foreigner ignored his own authority, as if the dean were a servant whose job it was to announce visitors to 'His Eminence'.

'Perhaps I should inform you that under this roof I am the sole authority.'

'Perhaps I should inform *you* who it is that sends this message,' answered the messenger, allowing himself the impertinence of imitating the dean's tone, while at the same time displaying the rubric and seal on the back of the envelope.

This forced the dean to promise that he would deliver the letter to the anatomist as soon as he returned from his travels.

ATEO COLOMBO'S FIRST IMPRESSION OF THE sick young woman was that she was infinitely beautiful and his second, that her illness was far from uncommon. Inés was lying in bed, apparently unconscious. He examined her eyes and her throat. He probed her head and inspected her ears, while the abbot followed the doctor's movements with distrustful curiosity. The anatomist felt her ankles and wrists and then begged the abbot to leave him alone with the patient, in the company of his 'apprentice', Bertino. Full of misgivings, the abbot left the room.

Mateo Colombo asked Bertino to help him undress the patient. For an untrained eye, it was difficult to guess that, under the austere dress, there hid a woman of such beauty – a discovery that caused the disciple's hands to shake like leaves with the removal of each article of clothing.

'Have you never seen a naked woman before?' Mateo Colombo asked Bertino somewhat maliciously, letting him

know, at the same time, that he, the anatomist, was as capable
of betraying him as the dean's own spy.

'Yes, I have . . . but not alive,' Bertino stammered.

'Let me remind you then that what you are seeing is not a
woman but a *patient*,' he said, stressing the difference between
the categories.

But Mateo Colombo himself was unable to ignore the
patient's beauty; being experienced, however, he betrayed no
emotion. He knew that a doctor had to rely on his subjective
impressions, and he guessed that his own unease was not
entirely unrelated to the patient's illness. He examined the
muscular tone of the belly and the rhythm of her breathing.
Seeing that Bertino was slow at his task, he ordered him to
complete at once the stripping of the patient. Then, just when
he was about to take the woman's pulse, Bertino uttered a cry
of horror:

'It's a man! It's a man!' he shouted, making the sign of the
Cross and calling out to all the saints in Heaven. 'God help
me!'

Mateo Colombo thought that Bertino had lost his senses.
The master rose and was about to try to calm his disciple when,
to his amazement, he saw between his patient's legs a perfectly
formed, erect and diminutive penis.

III

 HE ANATOMIST ORDERED HIS DISCIPLE TO stop shouting at once. Certainly the discovery, whatever it might be, put the already fragile life of his patient in great danger. Mateo Colombo remembered a case, fifty years earlier, in which a man had been led to the stake because he had the features of a woman, an aberration which had allowed him to work as a prostitute. Inés de Torremolinos's anatomy was fully female; her three daughters bore witness to her female physiology. And yet, in front of the astonished noses of the master and his disciple, was the small erect organ, pointing directly at their startled eyes, open wide like two pairs of gold florins.

The hypothesis that best explained the phenomenon was that the patient was a hermaphrodite. The ancient chronicles of Arab and Egyptian doctors told of numerous cases of creatures that displayed both sexes in the same body. The anatomist himself had been able to witness the case of a hermaphrodite dog. But this explanation did not take into account the facts. The common characteristic in such cases, set down in all the medical chronicles, was that these aberrations suffered from a total atrophy of the sexual organs, both male and female, making reproduction impossible. Not even considering the three daughters whom Inés de Torremolinos had brought into the world, the tiny organ was most obviously far from atrophied; on the contrary, it appeared to be inflamed, throbbing and moist.

Intuitively, the anatomist took hold of the strange organ between his thumb and index finger, and with the index finger of his other hand he began gently caressing the red and engorged gland. He then observed that every muscle in the patient's body, up to then completely relaxed, tensed suddenly and involuntarily, while the organ grew somewhat in size and throbbed with brief contractions.

'It moves!' cried out Bertino.

'Silence! Or do you want the abbot to find out?'

Mateo Colombo continued to rub the protuberance between his fingers, like someone rubbing a twig against a stone in order to make fire. Suddenly, as if he had finally managed to light a spark, Inés's entire body shook with one great convulsion that made her lift her hips and balance her body on her head and heels, like an arch. Gradually, her hips began to move to the regular rhythm of the anatomist's fingers. Her breathing became agitated, her heart was racing in her chest, and suddenly her entire body glistened with sweat. The anatomist's ministrations were provoking each of the dreadful symptoms that assaulted her every night. And yet, though the patient remained unconscious, it did not seem as if the proceedings were making her suffer exactly. Inés's breathing became hoarser and then broke into a loud panting. Her life-less features changed into a lascivious grimace, and the mouth, half open, revealed the tongue thrashing between the lips.

Bertino made the sign of the Cross. He was unable to tell whether this was an exorcism or if, on the contrary, his master was forcing the Devil into Inés's body. And he almost fainted when the patient suddenly opened her eyes, looked around and, now fully conscious, lent herself willingly to the anatomist's diabolical ceremony. Inés's nipples had grown red and erect and she herself began rubbing them with her own fingers, never taking her lascivious eyes off the stranger and muttering a few unintelligible words.

It appeared as if Inés had gone from her deathly agony to a *frenesi veneris*. Fully conscious of what was happening, or so it seemed, Inés gripped the bar at the head of her rustic bed. Between cries, convulsions and admonishing How-dare-yous, Inés allowed the anatomist to proceed.

'How dare you?' she would whisper, spreading her legs as far as possible. 'I'm a mother three times over!' rubbing her nipples. 'How dare you?' she'd implore again and let him carry on.

The anatomist's task was not an easy one. On the one hand, he had to remain aloof from the contagious arousal of his patient; on the other, he had to prevent the arousal from waning. And Bertino, making the sign of the Cross over and over again, continued to ask questions, crying out and even rebuking his master.

'You're committing a sacrilege, a profanation!'

'Shut up and hold down the arms!'

Confused as he was, Bertino obeyed.

'Not mine, you fool. The patient's!'

'How dare you?' Inés whispered. 'I'm a widow,' thrusting her hips against the anatomist's hand.

'How dare you?' she whimpered. 'You are two men and I'm one defenceless woman.' And she stretched her hand toward the assistant's member which, in spite of his calls to God, had begun to grow firm, thus thankfully ensuring for the anatomist Bertino's silence. 'How dare you?' Inés murmured. 'I've never cast eyes on you before.'

I V

OR TEN DAYS MATEO COLOMBO REMAINED in Florence by the side of his patient. Ten days during which Inés completely recovered, or at least recovered from her former affliction. The anatomist arranged with the abbot that he should lodge in one of the abbey cells, close enough to the patient's house so as not to interrupt his secret therapy. But Inés considered this to be an unpardonable breach of hospitality and put him up in her own house. And she prepared a comfortable bedroom for him, next to her own.

Inés was not the lascivious woman Mateo Colombo had come to know. On the contrary, she displayed all the conventional signs of saintliness: she was extremely plain in her dress, and reserved in her manner and her speech. However, when it was time to submit to the anatomist's therapy, it seemed as if a diabolical spirit rushed through her body, battering down the barriers of modesty, and that it withdrew only after she had reached the point of ecstasy, thereby allowing Inés to return to her decent ways. The patient appeared to struggle against the treatment with a few soft How-dare-yous which seemed more like groans of pleasure than cries of complaint. After the sessions, the performance was never mentioned, as if she kept no memory of it in her room or as if it had no more importance than taking a medicinal tea. As the treatment progressed, the mysterious penis-shaped protuberance decreased in size, together with the patient's suffering. And Inés appeared to enjoy Mateo Colombo's company. In the mornings they would walk along the hedge-lined path in the woods next to the abbey, and toward midday they would sit in the shadow of an oak tree to lunch on wild blackberries and strawberries. Mid-afternoon, Inés and the anatomist would return to the house, lock themselves up in her room and begin the treatment. Inés would obligingly lie back on the bed, lift her skirts over her legs, spread her knees and arch her back, allowing her soft and rounded thighs to balance in mid-air, and offer herself to the anatomist's hands, closing her eyes and pressing tight her lips still damp and stained with blackberry juice.

And every morning, Mateo Colombo and his patient would walk in the neighbouring woods, and in the afternoon they would enter the house, and she would whisper: 'How dare you, I've devoted my life to the Church even though I don't wear a nun's habit.' And every night, after a frugal and quiet dinner, she would moan: 'How dare you, I swore to remain chaste and celibate for the sake of my dear late husband's memory.'

Mateo Colombo felt at ease in Florence. The reason for remaining was not only to look after his patient's health. What was that tiny unnamed protuberance that behaved so like the male organ? What was that tiny monstrosity peering horribly from inside Inés's pubic regions? Was Inés a woman? Was she a monster of nature? Or was he, as he suspected, witnessing the most incredible discovery ever made within the mysterious female anatomy?

It was in those days, during his sojourn in Florence, that the anatomist wrote down the first notes that were to become the sixteenth chapter of his *De re anatomica*. Day after day, he described in his notebook the patient's progress.

Day the first:

Processus igitur ab utero exorti id foramen, quod os matricis vocatur illa praecipue sedes est delectionis, dum venerem exercent vel minimo digito attrectabis, ocyus aura semen hac atque illae pre voluptate vel illis invitis profluet.

This small protuberance, issuing from the uterus close to the aperture known as the matrix's mouth,[11] *is above all others the seat of the patient's delight; during sexual activity, rubbing the organ with only one finger, the semen*[12] *flows hither and thither faster than the air itself, driven by the feeling of pleasure and even without her will.*

[11] Of course, today we know that the organ in question does not 'issue from the matrix's mouth', as Thomas W. Laquier notes in his essay on Mateo Colombo, 'Amore Veneris, vel Dulcedo Apeletur', in *Fragments for a History of the Human Body*, Part One, edited by Michel Feher with Ramona Naddaff and Nadia Tazi, Zone, New York, 1989.
[12] Note that he writes 'semen', still attributing to the organ an eminently male character.

Day the second:

This female penis[13] appears to concentrate in itself all mani-festation of sexual pleasure to the detriment of the interior organs which do not betray a response when stimulated. It should be noted that this organ rises and falls like a penis before and after coitus or manual stimulation.[14]

Day the third:

The organ was hard and of oblong shape during my first exam-ination, and soft and fallen after the manipulation which led the patient to the frenesi veneris.

   The state of repose does not last long, rising again merely a few hours after the manipulations, even though the patient displays no signs of sexual appetite or frenzy, and does not seem inclined to pleasure, nor lustful for men or man's sexual organ. On the contrary, every time the organ rises, the patient appears melancholy, seized by dizzy spells and shortness of breath that cease only after manipulation and frenesi veneris.

[13] His manner of mentioning it is intriguing, since 'female penis' seems like a first attempt to universalize the 'anomaly', as he will say later on. In these early notes, the contradiction betrays Colombo's bewilderment.

[14] This note coincides almost exactly with that of Jane Sharp who, in *The Midwives Book*, London, 1671, wrote: ' . . . it rises and falls like a penis, and allows women to become excited and enjoy copulation.'

Day the fourth:

The patient is recovering. She no longer suffers from melancholy or shortness of breath, and her dizzy spells are less frequent. The organ remains less engorged and in a state of repose for longer periods. It is as if all her symptoms arose from this tiny bit of flesh. I will call this anomaly the Love or Pleasure of Venus (Amor Veneris, vel Dulcedo Apeletur).

Day the fifth:

It should be noted that the patient's love, disposition and will, seem to depend on this organ, and for that reason I am led to believe that whosoever controls this tiny organ will control her disposition and will. That is why the patient behaves toward me like a woman in love, showing herself eager to satisfy me in whatever it is I might desire. This organ appears to be the seat of the patient's love and pleasure. And such surrender does not depend on any attribute save that of knowing how to manipulate it with craft and cunning, and to recognize the sensitive parts, such as the tip and the lower crest of the elongated section.

Indeed, the anatomist knew how to take advantage of his 'craft and cunning'. Unabashedly, Mateo Colombo would complain to Inés of his meager pay as a teacher; he complained to her as his Genoese namesake had complained to his Queen: '*And I recalled to mind how little the twenty years of service have benefited me: I have no roof to call my own in my own land. If I*

*desire to sleep or eat, I must to the inn or the tavern, and at times
I lack even the coin to pay for my share. Shame and sorrow cleave
my heart.'* In a similar vein, the anatomist complained to his
patient. And Inés, charitable and compassionate, would feel
her heart crack with pity.

'Would five hundred florins be enough?' she would ask full
of shame, as if she were giving merely a few coins.

At night, after counting the last florin of his 'earnings', the
anatomist would write:

> *As the treatment advances, so too does the will of the patient
> become further ensnared; her readiness and obedience appear
> to have neither measure nor limit.*

Neither did the anatomist, after each session, appear to
have limit or measure. He missed no chance to bemoan his
misfortunes.

'Would a thousand florins be enough?' Inés would ask shyly.

All the passion which Inés had shown toward God Himself,
she now bestowed entirely on the anatomist. The verses she
once wrote to the Glory of the Almighty now had a new recip-
ient. At night, she went to bed thinking about the anatomist;
she dreamt of him, and his name was on her lips when she woke
in the morning. All her former concern for the poor, all her
charity and fervor, now carried a single name. And then came
the day of parting. According to her physician, Inés's health
was entirely recovered, and there was no longer a reason for
him to remain in Florence. The abbot warmly thanked the
chirurgo and his disciple for their services.

Inés's sickness now had a name: Mateo Renaldo Colombo.

Riding back to Padua, the anatomist's heart was beating anxiously. He had the intuition that something glorious had just taken place in his life.

IN THE LAND OF VENUS

I

*ARIAY, VERAGUA. THE GOLD MINES, THE infinite gold which people wear on their feet and arms, and which fills their coffers and their tables! The women wear gold wreaths from their head down to their shoulders. The Ganges is ten days' journey from here. From Cariay to Veragua the distance is the same as that from Pisa to Venice. I knew of all this, having read Ptolomy and the Scriptures. This is the place in which Paradise stood . . .'* Mateo Colombo could have written this, in the words his namesake had used to write to his Queen. *'O my America, my new-found-land!'* might have been better words to describe his adventure.

It would not take the anatomist long to realize that the strange and monstrous deformity he had discovered was in fact much like the fabled Indies of his namesake. On his return to Padua, he examined one hundred and seven other women, both alive and dead. To his astonishment, he realized that the 'penis' he had discovered on Inés de Torremolinos seemed to exist, 'small and hidden behind the fleshy labia', in all women.

And, to his delight, he discovered also that the small protuberance caused a behavior identical to that of Inés, both in
body and spirit. In pursuing his own quest as a lover, the
anatomist had, as if by chance, discovered the key to love and
pleasure. He was unable to explain how this 'sweet treasure'
had remained undetected for centuries, and how generations
of scholars, anatomists from the West and from the East, had
never seen that diamond that could be observed with the naked
eye simply by parting the flesh of the vulva.

'O my America, my new-found-land!' he might have written
in his *De re anatomica*. And then followed the exclamation with
an account of his discovery, told in the style of a symphonic
epic.

Between moans and cries of love, the anatomist caressed his
way along the coasts of his new world. Like copper-skinned
natives leaping from the green belly of the jungle, offering
themselves to the bearded men, half human and half beast,
women gave themselves to the new Master of the Land of
Venus. And he advanced, exploring the genital foliage, sword
in the right hand, the Scriptures in the left and the Cross
hanging from his neck. He advanced until one day he heard the
Voice of God instructing him: 'Give this thing a name.' And
in his diary, at the end of a day's work, he wrote: *'If I may be
allowed to give a name to the things by me discovered . . .'* And
then he named them. And he went on circumnavigating the
being created from his own rib.

Between moans and cries of love, he would kiss the sands of
his new world, pitching his banner, unable to find words to
describe so much novelty. His skill did not involve battling
native warriors. It was enough to point and say, 'this is mine',

and then, with the tip of his finger, a tiny finger (*minimo digito*), Wise and Cunning, the foliage would open for His Majesty to pass.

And he advanced, giving names and claiming what was his, as Adam's rib was part of Adam. Such gentle sweetness! And so he presented his findings to the world: 'This, dear reader, is the seat of love in women,' he said, pointing to the coast of the Land of Venus.

He lifted anchor and set sail toward canals and archipelagos where no man had yet set foot and, on the way, his index finger raised, he would remark: 'If the organ is rubbed with only one finger, the semen flows hither and thither faster than the air itself, driven by the feeling of pleasure and even without the woman's will.' And he would thus become Lord and Master of the female tides, making the waters open or close at his passing. He was the Governor, the Sovereign of the Will of Venus and, even without her consent, he would make her a slave to his Supreme Rule.

And he would bestow names with the blessings of St John and St Joseph. 'Call it matrix, uterus or vulva,' he would say, and proceed with the giving of names.

His ultimate destination had its own name already: Mona Sofia. There was no need to scour the world in search of a herb that would ensnare her perfidious heart. There was no need to call upon gods or demons. There was no need, even, to be gallant and practice the art of seduction. Here, at his disposal, and with no other requirement than to know how to rub wisely and skillfully, was the key to the heart of all women. He had discovered the anatomical cause of love. He was beating a path through which no man had ever walked before, toward that which, since the dawn of mankind, wizards, witches, rulers, dramatists and, indeed, any lovesick mortal had sought. Now he, the anatomist, Mateo Renaldo Colombo, had found it. Now at last, with his little finger, wise and cunning, he was Master of the land he had sworn to conquer: Mona Sofia.

And he was to go even further. If the female soul was a kingdom that could not be conquered by all the armies in the world, it was for a simple and evident reason which, because of its very transparency, no-one (no male, that is, of course) had ever noticed: the *Amor Veneris*, the root of female love, which irrefutably proved the fact that the female soul did not exist. And he would support this claim in *De re anatomica*.

But just as he who ventures into the lost inland valleys rarely finds his way back, the anatomist was to lose himself for ever in the impenetrable jungle of his own rib.

OOK XI, CHAPTER XVI OF *DE RE ANATOMICA* can be considered an epic, a true epic. As the statutes of the university demanded, on 16 March 1558, Mateo Colombo presented the dean with his finished work, a notebook of one hundred and fifteen pages illustrated by seven anatomical oil paintings in his own hand – in fact, one of the most beautiful books of the Renaissance – in which he laid out the maps of his new continent, the *Amor Veneris*.

On 20 March of that same year, Alessandro di Legnano entered Mateo Colombo's classroom accompanied by the priest of the university and two guards. The dean read out the ruling of the High Tribunal in which it was stated that Alessandro di Legnano's petition was granted, and that a Committee of Doctors would be formed to examine the activities of the anatomist and decide on the accusations levied against him of heresy, blasphemy, witchcraft and satanism. All his manuscripts were confiscated as well as the large number of paintings piled against the wall.

The fact that Mateo Colombo was not confined to a cell in the Prison of San Antonio should be attributed not to the benevolence of the authorities but to their desire that the hearing should not attract publicity before the committee's verdict. The anatomist was informed that, following Pope Paul III's bull concerning Doctoral Committees, in which these courts had been elevated to the rank of High Tribunals in matters of faith and accorded ambulatory faculties, the hearing would take place in the university itself. The tribunal would be presided over by Cardinal Caraffa and a delegate from Cardinal Alvarez de Toledo.

PART THREE

The Hearing

RAIN

I

ATEO COLOMBO, SITTING AT HIS DESK, watches the rain fall beyond the tiny moon-shaped window. It rains on the ten identical domes of the cathedral and on the fields that blend into the uncertain horizon. It rains such fine drops that it barely makes anything wet. It rains gently and persistently, like a wicked thought, or a doubt. Like an idea. Like a secret. It rains as if it is to rain throughout the centuries. It rains a pious, barefooted rain. It rains a Franciscan rain. It rains on the roofs and on the pigeons with the lightness of the saint's feet. It rains, as it always does, on the poor. It rains slowly but insistently, so that by its constant dripping it will wear away the marble feet of other, obscurantist saints. Not today or tomorrow. Soon, in a few days, black torches will burn, and embers will glow at the stake. But now it rains. It rains gently and persistently, like a warning or an omen. It rains kindly, charitably, refreshing the wound in the burnt flesh. It rains with a humming sound on the peasants who labor in the fields to feed the abbot and it rains on the ermine stole

of Pope Paul III. It rains on the Vatican Palace. And it also rains on the nuns, a warm, longed-for rain, with drops like tiny penises dripping down their necklines. It rains a fertile rain. A Latin rain.

Mateo Colombo watches the new rain as it falls. It rains and, in the depths of mud, the treasures of Antiquity are uncovered. It rains an archeological rain. And there, beneath the feet, antique splendor comes to light. It rains and through sheer rain, the historical ground is churned and spews up marbles, books and coins. Everything on the surface becomes, in comparison, trivial and vulgar. Under the maze of streets created by the demands of traffic, under the miserable slums, the water lays bare an Ancient and Splendid Empire. It rains and, from the guts of the earth, the Good, the Beautiful and the True are revealed. It rains and the *condottieri* dissolve into mud and in their place rise the spirits of Scipio, of Fabius.

Banished from his sweet new-found-land, from his Paradise, exiled in his cell, far, very far from his 'America', his motherland, Mateo Colombo watches the rain.

The anatomist watches the rain which, unless a miracle happens, will be his last.

O N 25 MARCH 1558, PRECEDED BY FIVE horsemen and followed by five guards, the committee chaired by Cardinal Caraffa and the delegate of Cardinal Alvarez de Toledo arrived in Padua. Their Eminences were lodged at the university, where they decided to take three days to examine the facts in the case before beginning proceedings. The dean offered Their Eminences the anatomical theater in which to establish their tribunal, but the visitors judged it too large for the court. The tribunal itself would consist of three judges – Cardinal Caraffa, the delegate Alfonso de Navas, and a representative of the Holy Office in Padua. The prosecutor would be the dean and, for his defense, the accused would have to rely on his own person. There would be only two or three witnesses present. Therefore Their Eminences judged that an ordinary classroom would provide them with more than sufficient space.

III

N 28 MARCH 1558 THE HEARING BEGAN. Following established precedent, the High Tribunal would first hear the witnesses for the prosecution, then the reading of the charges and, finally, the case for the defense. However, the tribunal deemed it improper to allow laymen to give their evidence in court and considered it more prudent to have the witnesses give written testimony before a notary public. Accordingly, the university's own official notary, Dario Renni, gathered the depositions.

THE DEPOSITIONS OF THE
WITNESSES

FIRST WITNESS

·

Deposition of a Harlot Who Declares Herself to Have Been
Put Under a Spell by the Anatomist

STANDING IN FRONT OF THE JUDGES, DARIO Renni read out
the first deposition.

'I, Dario Renni, notary at the University of Padua, hereby
proceed to take down the deposition of a harlot from the
brothel above the *Taverna del Mulo* who declares herself to be
named Calandra, to be seventeen years of age, and to live in the
above-mentioned quarters.

'The afore-mentioned declares that on the fourteenth day of
the month of June of the year of our Lord one thousand five
hundred and fifty-six, a stern-looking man arrived in the
brothel and demanded service. He was shown the pupils
working at the establishment and chose to employ one who
goes by the name of Laverda. The afore-mentioned declares
that he withdrew with her to a room, having paid only a small
sum, since this Laverda was old and somewhat ill; and that the

visitor eventually left the room without the harlot and quickly took his leave.

'The afore-mentioned declares that she felt much concerned for the other harlot who had not come out of the room and was not heard making any sounds. The above-mentioned declares that, since the other harlot failed to reappear, she entered the room and saw Laverda lying next to the bed. The afore-mentioned declares that at first she thought that the man was an unsatisfied customer who had taken his revenge because Laverda had not done her job properly, and because she was old and toothless. But she then saw that Laverda was breathing and that she bore no wounds, neither cuts of a blade nor bruises from a stick.

'The afore-mentioned declares that when Laverda awoke from her faint, she told her what had happened: that the client had given her his member to take into her mouth and when she had done this, she had seen that he was the Devil, demanding her love and her soul. The afore-mentioned declares that Laverda told her that she had traveled down Charon's river where fornicating demons possessed her with long tools through every orifice in her body, as a punishment for having been a loose woman all her life.

'The afore-mentioned declares that she paid no credence to Laverda's account, because she knew her to be a very old harlot who suffers from venereal madness.

'However, the following week, the visitor appeared once more above the tavern, requesting service, and once again he was shown all the pupils in the establishment, and this time he chose the afore-mentioned, who is an expensive harlot of young flesh. The afore-mentioned declares that the man was of refined demeanor and fierce eyes, very much to her liking, and that she went with him willingly and without complaint.

'The afore-mentioned declares that the visitor lifted his clothes above his waist and asked her to service his member which was hard and erect. The afore-mentioned declares that she did as her calling commands, artfully and with craft, and that, in so doing, she fell under the spell and cursed herself for not having heeded the words of Laverda.

'The afore-mentioned declares that the man was the Devil himself demanding her love and her soul; that she saw all manner of demons paying obeisance to the Evil One, and that all these great beasts were under the orders of their Master, placing their huge tools *contra natura* inside the afore-mentioned, thereby causing her much torment. And all the while she could hear the Beast-Master demanding that she render him her love and her soul, in order for the torment to cease. The afore-mentioned declares that the hellish Beast-Master demanded her love because she was a fallen woman, and claimed her soul belonged to him because she had made her living with her body. The afore-mentioned declares that she refused to give him her love in spite of the torment, having received the sacraments and knowing that her love and her soul belonged only to God.

'Having been shown the anatomist, Mateo Renaldo Colombo, the afore-mentioned declared that he was indeed the same man.'

Deposition of a Huntsman Who Declares Himself to Have
Seen the Anatomist in the Company of Demonic Beasts

I, DARIO RENNI, NOTARY AT THE UNIVERSITY OF PADUA,
hereby proceed to take down the deposition of a certain A.,
who declares himself to be twenty-five years of age, and to live
on a farmstead with his wife and four sons.

'The afore-mentioned declares that one day, having gone to
hunt in the woods in the vicinity of the abbey, he saw a man
walking in the company of a crow. The afore-mentioned
declares that the man was carrying a large bag on his shoulders
and in it he would collect whatever dead animals he would find
in his path, guided by the crow. The afore-mentioned declares
that such behavior attracted his attention and that, moved
by both curiosity and fear, he decided to follow him without
allowing himself to be seen, because the man seemed to be the
Devil himself. The man reached the ruins of an old abandoned
hut, and there he emptied his repulsive load. The afore-
mentioned declares that he saw, through one of the windows,

how the man fed the crow off the carrion. The afore-
mentioned declares that he also saw, to his horror, lying on the
table, several monstrous beasts: a dog with peacock feathers
and a cat covered in fish scales and that, after having been
touched by their master, these demons came to life and shook
and moved about as if possessed.

'Having been shown the anatomist, Mateo Renaldo
Colombo, the afore-mentioned declared that he was indeed the
same man.'

THIRD WITNESS

•

Deposition of a Peasant Woman Who Declares Herself to Have Been Bewitched by the Anatomist

I, DARIO RENNI, NOTARY AT THE UNIVERSITY OF PADUA, hereby proceed to take down the deposition of a certain B., who declares herself to be seventeen years of age and wife of C.

'The afore-mentioned occupies with her husband the farmstead next to the Main Lodge. The estate is administered by D. who confirms the above statement.

'The afore-mentioned declares under oath that she knows Messer Mateo Renaldo Colombo, whose faithful description she has provided. She also declares that she has been inside his university room of which she has also provided a detailed description.

'Asked how she came to know the anatomist, the afore-mentioned declares that she saw him for the first time in the company of Brother E., somewhere in the vicinity of the Main Lodge, beyond the hedges that border the farmstead. The afore-mentioned declares that after a long walk in the grounds of the workshops, the kitchen, the oven, the granary and the stables, the brother and the anatomist took leave of one another, the former walking toward the Main Lodge and losing himself among the hedges, the latter advancing toward the oven where the afore-mentioned was baking bread. The anatomist, after giving his name, asked her where her lord and master could be found. The afore-mentioned declares that, heeding to the anatomist's request, she went in search of her husband who was working on repairs at the abbey, because it was his day set aside for good works. The afore-mentioned declares that the anatomist then spent a long while speaking to her husband and that, in spite of not being able to hear their conversation, it seemed to her that she herself was the object of their discussion. The afore-mentioned declares that her husband then went in search of D., the steward of the estate, to whom they are indentured, and that these two remained talking for a while. The afore-mentioned declares that she saw the anatomist pay the steward some money, after which the steward authorized the afore-mentioned to leave the farmstead in the company and care of the visitor, Mateo Renaldo Colombo.

'The afore-mentioned declares that, under cover of darkness, she was led into the cellars of the university and there, surrounded by corpses, the anatomist asked her to undress and lie down on a cold slab of marble. The afore-mentioned declares that the doctor forced her to open her legs, whereupon he inserted a demon inside her. The afore-mentioned declares that in the midst of her ecstasy, she was unable to tear herself free because the demon inside her gave her more pleasure than she had ever felt before, while the anatomist ordered the Son of the Beast to charm the soul of the afore-mentioned, making her body burn like a furnace. The afore-mentioned declares she fell in love with the fierce demon and with the Wizard who drove him inside her body, guiding him by means of one finger. The afore-mentioned declares that from that day onwards she has been unable to enjoy her husband's *connubium*, because her body was still in the demon's power.

THE ACCUSATION

THE PROSECUTOR'S PLEA

•

Alessandro di Legnano's Accusation of Mateo Colombo
before the Committee of Doctors of the Church

'WE ARE WITNESSING THE RETURN OF THE DEVIL ON
Earth. You see him everywhere and anywhere. Wherever you
turn your head you will see nothing except the fruit of his
miserable labors. We are witnessing the conclusion of the
prophecy of St John, who saw the angel leading the Devil
away in chains and condemning him to a thousand years' exile
in the Abyss. Today, a thousand years later, the Devil has
returned. He is among us. Look! Look around you! Everyone
today seems to dig up the ancient gods. But are we to replace
the Holy Virgin with Venus? Are we to raise Bacchus above
St John the Baptist? Just look at our churches, cluttered with
the ancient pagan gods! Therefore I ask you: what can we
expect from the rest of humanity if the very House of God
has become the abode of the Devil? Listen to the vulgar
talk in the piazzas and the fairs, and tell me if there is a
difference between that idle gossip and the prose of the

new 'intellectuals' who are ignorant even of Latin and Greek. Indolence, an easy conscience, vulgar anecdotes, jibes and all kinds of obscenities add up to what today we call literature. Beware! The Devil is among us! This is the hour in which the son will rebel against the father, the disciple against the teacher. You ought to see the horde of would-be anatomists in the university I have been chosen to preside over: they have refused to swear the oath of their trade. No-one listens any more in respectful silence to the learned, the students mock us to our very faces. If you could hear with what levity they speak of God Himself – with the same frigid detachment with which they speak of growing vegetables! Anyone can now declare himself an atheist, with the ease of someone choosing one dish over another. But I say to you: Beware! The Devil has freed himself from his chains and is among us once again.

'Today the Devil wears the gown of science. Today false prophets proclaim themselves scientists and artists. Are we to wait idly for these new painters, sculptors and anatomists to replace our Lord Jesus Christ with marble statues of Lucifer above the pulpits?

'It falls on us, Christian men, to distinguish Truth from Travesty.

'I accuse the prisoner of perjury, because he has broken his oath. Let me remind you of the observances he swore to keep on the day on which he received his medical degree:

I swear, as God is my witness, to comply in the measure of my capabilities and according to my best judgement with the following oath and covenant: I will look upon him who shall

have taught me this Art even as one of my parents. I will share
my substance with him, and I will supply his necessities, if he
be in need. I will regard his offspring even as my own brethren,
and I will teach them this Art, if they would learn it, without
fee or covenant. I will impart this Art by precept, by lecture
and by every mode of teaching, not only to my own sons but to
the sons of him who has taught me, and to disciples bound by
covenant and oath, according to the Law of Medicine.

The regimen I adopt shall be for the benefit of my
patients according to my ability and judgement, and not for
their hurt or for any wrong. I will give no deadly drug to
any, though it be asked of me, nor will I counsel such, and
especially I will not aid a woman to procure abortion.
Whatsoever house I enter, there will I go for the benefit of
the sick, refraining from all wrongdoing or corruption, and
especially from any art of seduction, of male or female, of
bond or free. Whatsoever things I see or hear concerning the
life of men, in my attendance on the sick or even apart there-
from, which ought not to be noised abroad, I will keep silence
thereon, counting such things to be as sacred secrets. In con-
sequence, may it be granted to me, if I remain faithful to my
oath and not break it, to enjoy my life and my Art,
celebrated among mankind. But if I were to break it and
thereby commit perjury, let the contrary befall me.

'I accuse the prisoner of perjury, having broken every single
word of his oath, dishonoring and profaning the office for
which he was instructed in this House.

'I accuse the prisoner of satanism and witchcraft. Anything
I might say is little compared to the proofs offered by the

prisoner himself. You have heard the depositions of the witnesses, you have read the documents in the case and you have seen the paintings which the prisoner executed with his own hands. But the most conclusive proof is the prisoner's own word. The discovery he claims is nothing but a diabolical deceit. What else can we call this *Amor Veneris*? The prisoner claims to have discovered the organ that rules over the will, love and pleasure of women, as if the will of the soul and the pleasure of the body could be considered equals. What else but diabolical can we call he who pretends to elevate the Devil to the summits that belong only to God?

'Looking at the matter from a strictly anatomical point of view, what is this so-called *Amor Veneris*? Words, merely words. You can search and hunt in the female genitalia and you shall find no such *Amor Veneris*, no organ not described already by Rufus of Ephesus, Avicenna or Julius Polux. Perhaps the *Amor Veneris* is another name for the *nymphae* noted by Berengarius, or for the *praeputio matrices* described in the tenth century by the Arab Hali–Abbas. I say to you: words, nothing but words. Perhaps the prisoner's "discovery" is the *tentigenem* mentioned by Abulcassis? All words, diabolical words.

'But I shall leave the accusation to the prisoner himself. Hear his defense and you shall find in his own words proof of what I speak.'

THE DEFENSE

I

PRIL THIRD WAS THE DATE ON WHICH THE accused was to present his case. Mateo Colombo entered the room in which the High Tribunal had set up court armed with nothing but his own beliefs. He was wearing a woolen *lucco*, a shawl over his shoulders and a *foggia* covering his head and forehead, which he took off as he stood facing the bench. To the right of the judges sat his accuser, Alessandro di Legnano. Cardinal Caraffa reminded him of the charges against his person and, this formality over, ordered him to proceed with his defense.

All eyes fell on the sorrowful figure of the anatomist. Standing in front of the judges, he seemed unable to find words to speak; during his captivity, he had tried out so many addresses that now not a single one came to his assistance.

II

Mateo Renaldo Colombo's Plea before the Committee of
Doctor's of the Church

'EVEN THOUGH THESE CIRCUMSTANCES DON'T APPEAR TO
be either the best suited or the most appropriate, I wish to
begin by stating that it is a great honor shown toward my
humble person, that Your Excellencies should deign to listen
to the words I am about to pronounce. I say this with the
intimate conviction that, in happier circumstances than those
granted to me by fate, you yourselves would have welcomed
my work and my discovery and taken them under your ines-
timable protection. I am one who believes that matters related
to the body should be demonstrated, first and foremost, from
a theological viewpoint, for nothing exists outside God. My
calling, that of anatomy, consists of deciphering the work of
the Almighty and, in this manner, I worship His handicraft.
You, learned theologians, are wise not only through faith but
also through reason. Not one word which you read in my

work has a reason beyond that of faith. With this I mean that
the Scriptures are for me not only printed paper; every time
I am given to examine a body, I see in it the work of the
Almighty and on every inch of that body I read the Divine
Words, and my spirit is moved.

'Before pleading my case, allow me to say that I haven't lost
hope that, after hearing my words, you will take under your
learned protection the discovery that was granted me, as well
as the testimonials of my *De re anatomica*.

'I realize that some of my conclusions, in the mouth of my
accuser, may appear as preposterous daydreams, and that
from my anatomical studies might be deduced certain other
concepts that may appear as morally dubious. I mean to say:
to present a thesis on the body implies, inevitably, another
thesis concerning the soul. My discoveries are anatomical; if,
by describing the functions of the organs, I appear to be laying out a metaphysical doctrine, I must leave it to the
philosophers to disentangle one from the other. I, in all
modesty, am nothing but a humble anatomist whose purpose
is no other than to interpret the work of the Almighty and, in
this manner, to praise Him.

'I hasten therefore to say, as I am convinced you will
conclude with me when I have come to the end of my plea, that
nothing of what is written in *De re anatomica* and nothing of
what I am about to expound in your presence contradicts in
any way the Holy Scriptures and that, on the contrary, their
Truth has always been my inspiration.

'Allow me then, in order to structure my exposition
and render it as intelligible as my meager skills will permit,
to divide my plea into nineteen sections.

FIRST SECTION

Concerning Why the Kinesis Is Not an Attribute of the Soul but of the Body

'ALLOW ME TO TAKE A SHORT BYWAY INTO A NUMBER OF questions related to the body and its elemental functions, and to lay before you certain relationships which I have been able to establish.'

The anatomist, standing in front of the bench, took a long and deliberate pause, in an attempt to gather the undivided attention of the committee members.

'Please humor me by observing for a moment the automata yonder,' he said, pointing in the direction of the window, outside which the clock tower could be clearly seen; at that precise moment, as if prearranged, the bells began to strike, 'and notice the movement of those bronze figures,' he insisted, claiming not only the doctors' attention but also suggesting that his will had caused the carillon to start. 'Observe the figures striking the bells and observe also the clock they are surrounding. Because it is of this that I wish to speak: of movement. I will begin by saying that the principle that governs that precise, punctual machinery is not in the slightest different from the principle that governs the movement of our own bodies.

'Just like those clockwork figures, we are made out of matter, and that matter must take on a form. And, just like the matter of those mechanical creatures, our matter is animated by some form of *kinesis* that lends it movement. This is a borderline point between anatomy and philosophy, because it might appear that the question of what governs the movement of a body requires, in fact, a metaphysical answer.

'It is a well-known fact that the soul governs the movements of the body; you are not teaching us anything new . . .

'You force me to leap ahead of myself. I am sorry I must contradict you but, in my opinion, the soul has no say in these mechanics, just as the soul has no say in the movements of the clock. But I beg you to let me continue in the order I had established. Before giving you my opinion on the soul, I wish to lay before you another discovery which, fortunately, no-one has thought it necessary to question. I refer to my discovery of pulmonary circulation. In my account of the phenomenon, I've described how the blood is pressed into the cavities of the heart when it is dilated and, searching an exit toward a larger space, it passes with great force from the right cavity into the arterial vein, and from the left cavity into the major artery. When, after the dilation, the heart contracts again, new blood enters from the *vena cava* into the right cavity and from the left vein into the other. There exist, at the mouth of the four canals, small fleshy organs that allow the entry of blood mainly through the latter, and its exit mainly through the former.'

SECOND SECTION

Concerning the Kinetic Fluids

'NOW ALLOW ME TO DESCRIBE TO YOU HOW THE DIFFERENT parts of the body are endowed with movement and you shall see how the government of muscular *kinesis* depends not on the soul but on the body. Allow me to introduce to you the tiny corpuscles that inhabit the blood and that I have called *"kinetic fluids"*.[15] These are the fluids that, traveling at great speed, pass from the blood coming from the brain into the nerves connected to the muscles. Muscles betray only two kinds of movement: contraction and dilation. In order for a muscle to stretch, there has to be a corresponding muscle that must contract and both, in different proportions, must have received these fluids from the brain. I don't mean any kind of metaphysical cause because these *"kinetic fluids"*, as I have said, are made of matter. And it is precisely this matter that fills or empties the muscles in order for these to contract or dilate. This and no other is the principle on which movement is based. I must add, however, that what I have just described is only the beginning of *kinesis*. I still must illustrate for you the constitution of the nerves responsible for directing this mechanical procedure, lending order to chaos. The following exposition shall be, at the same time, my defense regarding the deposition of one of Your Excellencies' witnesses,' he said, turning to the dean, 'in whose account I am accused of being accompanied, God forbid, by certain demonic beasts.'

[15] The 'kinetic fluids' described by Mateo Colombo are surprisingly similar to what Descartes would call 'animal spirits' in his *Traité des passions*. It would not seem unlikely that the French philosopher drew his inspiration from Mateo Colombo.

THIRD SECTION

Concerning the Demonic Beasts

THE ANATOMIST WENT TO HIS SEAT AND RETURNED TO the bench with a bag on his shoulder.

'This is the bag the huntsman saw,' he said, lifting it toward the bench, 'and indeed, it is no secret that every morning I venture into the woods next to the farm and collect the bodies of animals which I later dissect and examine. I don't wish to distract your attention from the subject of my exposition. But allow me to illustrate what I have just explained regarding movement,' he said, and proceeded to untie the knot that held the bag. At that point, the huntsman who had given his deposition and who was sitting in the room together with the other witnesses, stood up and, nervously, asked to be excused. His request was, of course, denied.

The doctors watched the anatomist with some concern, as a murmur grew in the room. Mateo Colombo put his hand inside the bag and when he drew it out and exhibited the contents, the murmur became a cry of horror and the huntsman broke out in terrified alarm:

'That is the demon, one of the ones I saw! To the stake! Take him to the stake!'

The anatomist was holding by its legs a truly horrendous beast. It had the aspect of a wolf with large fangs showing from behind snarling lips. Instead of hair, the beast had red feathers on its head which lent it the appearance of a being in flames. The rest of the body was covered in golden scales and on its back it had two dorsal fins, like a fish. Just as the anatomist was about to place it on the floor, the beast unfolded a pair of wings and let out a lion's roar. The witnesses and even the judges were about to run for their lives, and no doubt Mateo Colombo would have been attacked there and then, if anyone had dared go near him.

'Be not afraid. This is the beast the witness mistook for a demon. As you can see, it is made of lifeless matter,' he said, exhibiting it to the committee, 'and it can do nothing of its own free will, since it has no life of its own. I made this creature myself. Look here. This is merely an old stuffed wolf whose skin I shaved; instead of hair, I inserted cock's feathers and colored fish scales in its pores. And these wings and fins are sewn on with needle and thread.'

'We all saw it move on its own and heard it let out a roar!'

'That, indeed, is my exposition. If you will allow me, I will explain, using this artificial beast, how movement is produced. No-one would imagine that the clockwork figures who strike the bells every hour are demonic beasts. Neither is this. The principle governing its movements is the same as the one that governs theirs,' he said, pointing once again toward the window. 'Now look!'

The anatomist grabbed the animal by the scruff of the neck and, holding it in his arms, manipulated something that jutted from its belly. He placed it on the floor and, once again, the room filled with cries of fear. The beast had begun waddling here and there, beating its wings madly and letting out terrifying roars.

'You have nothing to fear! It will do you no harm!'

'Stop that demonic beast at once! Stop it I say!'

Obeying the order, the anatomist grabbed his beast by the

neck, touched once again its belly and it fell as still and rigid as a corpse. Holding it by its legs, Mateo Colombo proceeded:

'As you can see, the *kinesis* does not depend at all on the soul. This artificial beast can walk, emit sounds and beat its wings, just like a real animal. This beast which, obviously, does not exist anywhere in nature, is a good though rudimentary imitation of the principle that governs movement, including the movement of our own bodies. My purpose in fashioning such a beast is none other than to prove the truth of my theories.'

FOURTH SECTION

Concerning Automata

'I WILL NOW DEMONSTRATE HOW MY BEAST FUNCTIONS. AS I have explained, the nerves act on the muscles granting them movement,' and the anatomist uncovered in the beast's belly a small bronze handle hidden among the scales, which he pulled to open a hinged panel. 'Our nerves are made up of a couple of elements: the exterior skin and the interior marrow. The former acts as a sort of covering or lining over the latter. A muscular contraction is only the effect of the nerves retracting. Just as when we pull one end of a rope, anything tied to the other end is forced to follow. That is how our muscles move. Our body contains innumerable nerves that direct even the subtlest of our movements. I have modestly reproduced this principle here by creating twenty artificial nerves, made out of lengths of thread encased in tripe, in order to obtain twenty different movements. The principle is identical to that of the machinery inside a clock,' he said, exposing to the tribunal the open belly of the automaton. 'Here you can see the spring that retracts onto itself and that, when freed, transmits its movement through the threads to all the movable parts. Of course, this is but a rough imitation, but it serves to illustrate quite accurately the point I'm trying to make. I've built about ten of these automata following the principles I've been able to observe in living bodies, as well as in the interior architecture of corpses.'

'Just listen to how this anatomist sets himself up as the Almighty, pretending to emulate the work of the Creator,' shouted the dean, jumping from his chair and pointing at the accused.

'Your Excellency is mistaken,' Mateo Colombo answered meekly. 'We anatomists only interpret the Almighty's Work and, as far as we can shed light among the shadows, we merely adore our Creator. Science, as I conceive it, is the method by which we understand and pay homage to His handiwork. My very modest machineries are only clumsy travesties compared to the Work of the Almighty, and have no other purpose than to render understandable at least a small fragment of His Creation.'

'Words, mere words,' the dean interrupted. 'You have heard with your own ears the confession of the accused,' continued Alessandro di Legnano with a sneer: 'The anatomist has admitted that to cobble together his puppets he has made use of foul corpses. I do not need to remind you that a bull of Our Holy Father, Boniface VIII, which has never been revoked, forbids the dissection of cadavers.' The dean beamed triumphantly.

'I thank Your Excellency for agreeing with me that my animal is indeed no demonic beast, as he maintained until now, and only a harmless doll. This is what I intended to demonstrate. Therefore the prosecutor has himself rejected the deposition of his own witness.'

Again purple with anger, the dean was unable to find an objection and glared instead at the huntsman, as if he were responsible for the defendant's words.

'As for the bull mentioned by Your Excellency, allow me to correct you. In it there is no prohibition on "dissecting cadavers", as you infer, but only on "obtaining cadavers for dissection", which is something quite different. May I remind you why Our Holy Father wisely forbade such practices, not of dissection, I insist, but of obtaining the dead bodies. Your Excellency, I am certain, knows full well that it all began at the university over which you now preside and precisely with the chair of anatomy that I was elected to fill. At the time, the chair was occupied by Marco Antonio della Torre and you no doubt remember the disruption he caused. Who, in fact, can forget the accounts of those days? Marco Antonio professed an unqualified atheism. He practiced the dissection of cadavers without any moral reservations, condoning even criminal behavior. It is true that he himself would prompt his apprentices to obtain cadavers by any possible means, not only buying them from executioners and gravediggers, but also stealing them from hospital morgues and even taking them down from the gallows. It has also been said that they plundered graves, sometimes choosing their targets while still alive as if they were lambs about to be roasted. But you know full well that is not so in my case. You know how jealously I caution my students against unorthodox dissections and how the cadavers I use come only from the morgue. You also know that before I cut into a dead human body, I first dissect dozens of animal bodies. And, as you can now ascertain for yourselves, my "demonic beast" has not a single human bone in its body.'

FIFTH SECTION

Concerning Bodies Both Living and Dead

'UP TO THIS POINT I HAVE DESCRIBED FOR YOU THE mechanics of the body and, as you will surely agree, these mechanics do not differ substantially from the principle governing the clock tower automata. And now I say to you: the soul has no part in the movement of the body.'

'Do you dare insinuate that *kinesis* is not an attribute of the soul?'

'No, I do not insinuate it, I affirm it most categorically. *Kinesis* is not governed by the soul. This error can be demonstrated by simply observing a corpse. When we look at a corpse, we may come to the mistaken conclusion that the cause of death is nothing but the absence of the soul. And yet, I say that heat and movement depend only on the body. For example, observe that animal,' he said, fixing the dean with his eyes, and then pointing to the back of the room where a cat was tearing apart a cockroach. 'Observe its precise movements, so much more precise even than ours, and see how the soul has no bearing on the *kinesis*, unless you intend to bestow a soul upon that animal,' still pointing at the cat but without taking his eyes off the dean.

The dean, furious, was unable to refute this. And, seeing that no-one was able to raise any intelligent objections, the anatomist continued:

'The soul leaves upon the arrival of death and only because of the corruption setting in on the organs responsible for the movement of the body. So it is that the body does not die for lack of a soul, but through the corruption of a few or all of its organs. And now that I have spoken to you about how the body functions, allow me to speak of the soul that inhabits it.'

SIXTH SECTION

Concerning the Passions of the Soul and the Actions of the Body

'AS I HAVE ALREADY SPOKEN TO YOU OF THE BODY, ALLOW me to continue to refer to it in order to reveal its soul. I have said that *kinesis* is not a function of the soul but exclusively one of the body. Following this path, I dare venture further and say that in order to distinguish the soul from the body we are obliged to differentiate between that which pertains to movement and that which does not. If you agree with me that the soul has no commerce with physical things but only with things metaphysical, you must allow me that

movement, *kinesis*, is a branch of physics that relates exclusively to the material world. This *kinesis* governs our body's
movement. And if, in order to differentiate the things of the
soul from those of the body, we set the actions of the body
against the immaterial things of the soul, we shall encounter
the so-called passions. I will define as "passion" all those faculties of the will that bear no relation to the body, that are
born and die in the soul itself without the body's intervention. That is to say, faculties that exist passively in the soul
and never actively in the body, and that proceed from no
organ but from the soul itself, and produce no change except
in that very same soul. I distinguish between actions and
passions, in the pure sense of these words, since there are also
passions that are born in the soul but which affect the movement of the body. Even these passions must, however, be
distinguished from actions because, even though they produce certain bodily movements, these have no other purpose
outside the scope of the soul, as for instance when the soul
wishes to express its love for God through prayer. You can
see how, in this case, the body is but a means for the soul to
manifest itself, and the purpose of this action is governed
exclusively by the soul. In the same way, but in inverse ratio,
there are bodily actions, born in the body and aimed at the
body, in which the soul intervenes between the beginning of
the action and its end. This is the case with those sinful oc-
casions which the soul might wish to avoid, for instance,
when the sexual organs are stimulated and the soul intervenes
in order to prevent a sin of the flesh, or when we have
promised to fast and the digestive organs clamor for food, and
the soul intervenes to resist the temptation of eating.'

SEVENTH SECTION

Concerning Love and Sin

'NOTHING WILL BETTER ILLUSTRATE MY EXPOSITION THAN the subject of love. We believe, erroneously, that the passions lead us to the sin of the flesh. The temptation that drives us to this sin has nothing to do with the passions, but with the bodily actions, since this is a sin whose origin lies in the body. We should therefore differentiate love, which is purely an attribute of the soul, from the sexual impulse. Love is a passion, because it finds its source and its end in the soul itself, while the sexual impulse begins and comes to term in the body. There is no organ that either breeds or extinguishes love, but the sexual impulse has a bodily location, both in its beginning and in its end. And you will concur with me that the purest of all loves is that which we feel for God.'

EIGHTH SECTION

Concerning the Anatomy of Women and the Morals of Men

'NOW ALLOW ME TO EXPLAIN ONE OF THE PREMISES THAT guided my pen in the writing of *De re anatomica*, the conclusion of many years of study. I once said that "If moral science studies the behavior of men, anatomy should claim for its field of study the behavior of women." In order to explain these words, allow me to quote the great Aristotle. You will no doubt recall Aristotle's authoritative teachings regarding procreation. He says, in his *Metaphysics*, that the union of both sexes allows for reproduction in the following manner: the male semen lends the child being formed its identity, essence and idea, while the woman lends it only the matter that will fashion the future child's body. And the great Aristotle says that semen is not a material fluid but that it is wholly metaphysical. As the Greek Master has taught, man's sperm is the essence, the essential power that transmits life to the future being. Man carries in his semen the breath of life, the form, the identity that turns matter into a living thing. Semen has the movement given to it by its creator; it is the execution of an idea that matches the father's shape, without the transmission of matter. In ideal conditions, the future being will have the complete identity of its father, since "Semen is an *organon* that possesses movement in action . . . Semen is not a part of the gestating fetus."[16] Just as no material particle passes from the carpenter to the object he creates, to be part of the wood, in the same way no particle of semen takes part in the constitution of the embryo; just as music is not the instrument and the instrument is not the music. And yet, music is identical to the musical idea in the composer's mind.'

[16] Aristotle, *Metaphysics*, Bk VII, 9, 1034b.

NINTH SECTION

Concerning the Inexistence of Women's Souls

'WHAT I MEAN TO SAY IS THAT, IF WE CARRY ARISTOTLE'S concept to its logical conclusion, we shall see that there is no reason to believe that there exists in women such a thing as a soul.'

The anatomist's last comment provoked a wave of murmuring in the room. Various signs of agreement could be seen here and there and even an involuntary nod of assent from among the Committee of Doctors.

'Anathema!' roared the dean, jumping to his feet. 'Who other but Satan himself would pronounce such words!' He was about to continue, but realized that not one idea was coming to his rescue. He had never thought that, one day, he would have to attempt a defense of women and, in fact, he had not a single favorable opinion of the opposite sex. The dean hated women, as Mateo Colombo knew well. So he took advantage of the dean's long silence, looking at him as if impatient to hear his views on the matter. But 'You are offending the Holy Virgin's Blessed Name,' was the strongest argument the dean could come up with.

'May I remind you that the miracle of birth is forbidden to man? The Conception of Christ was a miracle performed by God on the person of Mary. But you can't pretend that all women conceive as Mary did. Your Excellency no doubt knows that Our Lady is the One and Only, as is the One and Only Christ, the Son of God. And if the Son of God possessed a body when on this Earth, that body was given to him by

Mary. Of course I am not speaking of the miracle of Mary. But take instead the example of Eve. Would you worship Eve in the same way as you worship Our Lady? Your Excellency must recall that God punished Eve in her daughters for all generations and that, even after Mary, the daughters of Eve give birth in pain. You must not confuse the holy exception with the rule of those punished for Eve's original sin. And I ask, in the words of St Gregory, "What is woman but the will of the flesh?"'

TENTH SECTION

Concerning the Dark Ways of Women

'EVERYTHING I HAVE SAID ABOUT THE SOUL CONCERNS only men, not women. This is why I say to you that, if we are to understand the dark ways of women by following the path of moral philosophy, we shall reach no result whatsoever, for they lack a soul. And that is why I say to you that the only path that will lead us to an understanding of women's behavior is the path of anatomy. I have no doubts about this since, as a result of my extensive investigations, I have been able to discover an organ which exists in the female anatomy and that fulfills the function of the soul in men, and whose effects can be easily confused with what I have called "the passions". I mean to say that there are no such passions in women, but only actions which begin and end in their own body. The volition that governs female behavior is born in the female body and, more precisely, in the organ I have mentioned. Certain metaphysicians and certain anatomists as well have sought to discover where in the body the soul might find its nesting-place. I tell you that the soul does not reside in the body but that it flutters around it like an angel. As far as women are concerned, if you wish to find in them something equivalent to the male soul, you must look for it inside their body, the dwelling-place of demons. And I tell you that this demon which has its house inside the female body, resides precisely inside the organ of which I shall now speak. And I will venture to say that, if we succeed in explaining the mechanics of this organ, we will at last be able to explain the dark ways of women themselves.'

ELEVENTH SECTION

Concerning the Existence of a Female Organ Which I Have Called Amor Veneris *and Which Is Comparable to the Soul of Man*

'THERE EXISTS IN THE FEMALE BODY AN ORGAN THAT performs similar functions to those of the soul in men, but whose nature is utterly different, since it depends entirely on the body.

'This organ is, first and foremost, the seat of women's delight. This protuberance that issues from the uterus, close to the opening known as the "mouth of the matrix", is the beginning and end of all actions destined to provoke sexual pleasure. During sexual activity, and not only when rubbed with a penis but even when touched with a finger, the

semen[17] flows freely faster than the air itself, driven by the
feeling of pleasure and even without the woman's will. If this
part of the uterus is touched when the woman is in heat and
in a frenzy of lust, it appears to be harder and of an oblong
shape, to the point of resembling the male member – but I
will return to this later on. And as no-one before me has discovered this protuberance or studied its use, if I may be
allowed to give a name to the things by me discovered, I wish
it to be called *Amor Veneris*.

'And I categorically declare that it is in this organ that
women's actions find their root, as well as all that might
resemble male passions. I mean to say that woman is governed by this *Amor Veneris* and that all her actions, from the
most noble to the most repugnant, from the most worthy and
honorable to the most vile and despicable, have no other
source than this organ. From the most promiscuous strumpet
to the most faithful and chaste wife, from the most devout
and consecrated nun to the crone who practices witchcraft, all
women, without exception, are under the influence of this
anatomical part.'

TWELFTH SECTION

Concerning the Moral Frailty of Women

'NOW I WILL EXPLAIN HOW THIS ORGAN WORKS AND WHY
it produces in every woman a different behavior. And if you

[17] Mateo Colombo's name for the female flow.

interpret my words to be an attack against women, you are much mistaken because, just as man proceeds according to his free will in virtue of the soul that was given him, woman is not the mistress of her own actions, but slave to the whims of her *Amor Veneris*. To this alone do I attribute the frailty of her morals, as we shall see further on.'

THIRTEENTH SECTION

Concerning the Reason Why Male Semen Is of a Metaphysical Nature and Why It Is Able to Propel Itself by Its Own Means

'I HAVE EXPLAINED TO YOU MY THEORY OF *KINETIC FLUIDS*. These act very much as the will; by this, I mean that they direct the bodily actions so that the body does not perish, actions such as feeding, evacuation, etc. I have also said that in a body governed by a soul, sinful actions are diverted from the path toward which they are directed by their source, that is to say, the body. I now want to talk to you about the course of these *kinetic fluids* which, being produced in the brain, must naturally be evacuated from the body so as not to poison it. I have discovered that the body maintains a constant volume of these fluids and that the usual procedure by which these are evacuated is by evaporation. In any given movement,' and here the anatomist flexed his arm several times, 'the fluid that reaches the muscle to contract or extend it, evaporates at the moment of action through the heat which this movement produces. This occurs in the simplest actions; but in the more complex ones, in which the soul must intervene, matters become some-what more tangled. During sexual desire, when the impulse to copulate is born, the body produces a large quantity of *kinetic fluids* that travel, according to the procedure I've described, toward the sexual organs, assisting in the dilation of the veins and the relaxation of the muscles, to allow the blood to enter the male member and become erect. Semen, as Aristotle has said, is of a metaphysical nature but it requires a material component to jettison it. This material component of the semen, which is the one we can see, is simply the *kinetic fluid* in its pure state. Nothing else can explain why it leaps with the energy of lava from a volcano. Semen's function is not only to guide the spirits but also to free the body of the *kinetic fluids* produced during intercourse, which, if retained by the body, would poison it, making it dangerously sick. Now, what becomes of these fluids when their action is halted through the will of the soul?'

FOURTEENTH SECTION

Concerning the Soul and Sexual Appetites

'ACCORDING TO THE MECHANICAL PROCESS I HAVE HAD the good fortune of observing, sexual appetite occurs in man when the organs of sight or touch are aroused by a tempting and sinful external object, such as a woman or the image of a woman (it is easy to ascertain that the painting of a beautiful woman produces the same effect). This arousal that affects the external nerves (in the eye, for instance) frees the *kinetic fluids* from their prison in the muscles, allowing them to travel to the

brain like a messenger. There, inside the brain, more *kinetic
fluids* are produced, which in turn travel to the sexual organs,
as I have said, engorging the male member and inciting the
muscles necessary for intercourse. Most of these fluids are
deposited in the testes and in the member, in the form of
semen. This is when the soul intervenes and censures the
action. But since semen is, as I have said, of a metaphysical
nature, most of its volume is made out of pure spirit. If you
observe a sample of semen some time after it has been
produced, you will see that it reduces to a tenth of its original
volume. This is because the spirits that inhabited it have
returned to their place in the soul. Therefore, when the soul
puts an end to sinful actions, it transforms these actions of the
body into passions of the soul. How else can we explain the fact
that, when we pray fervently to God in order to avoid temptation, the sexual appetite will be totally extinguished and the
member will return to its relaxed position, having previously
been full of seminal fluid? If you fill a gut with water until it is
completely bloated, it will not return to its flaccid state unless
you pour out the water or burst the gut through excessive pres-
sure. But we can observe that this does not occur in the case of
the male member which, thanks to the intervention of the soul,
can return to its position of repose without expelling its semen,
that is to say, without having reached the conclusion intended
by the sinful action. The metaphysical nature of semen is
obvious, since it is the only fluid (not counting blood) that does
not need to be drained. It would not be possible to postpone
indefinitely the evacuation of urinary and fecal matter; semen,
on the other hand, does not need to be expelled after having
been produced. We should not feel ashamed of having been

drawn to temptation; on the contrary, the more times we have been able to free ourselves from it, the greater and more numerous will be the passions of our soul.'

FIFTEENTH SECTION

Concerning the Sexual Appetite of Women and the Absence of a Guide to the Soul

'BUT WHAT TAKES PLACE IN A WOMAN'S BODY WHEN SHE becomes aroused and desirous of a male member, since she lacks a soul to transform the seminal fluids produced by such actions into soulful passion? Woman's semen is much heavier and thicker than that of man, because among its particles there are no spirits; it therefore consists purely of *kinetic fluids*. The process of sexual arousal in a woman is different from that in man. I have said that the process begins, in men, in the sensitive organs aroused by a sinful object, that is to say, a woman. So it is that man is the subject of the enticement while woman is the object of temptation. In the same way that one thing cannot be also its contrary, the subject cannot also simultaneously be the object. What I mean to say is that the process of sexual arousal in a woman does not begin in the sensory organs through casting eyes on a man, but it is born spontaneously and naturally, and has its origin within the body and, more precisely, in the organ I have described for you. Woman is always the object of sin. What I am laying before you in anatomical terms is hardly new in moral terms: here you have,

once again, the example of Eve, object of temptation, whose
subject is Adam. But I will refer back to this point later. Allow
me to continue my thesis on the origin and destiny of sexual
appetite in women. The sexual impulse, which occurs naturally and spontaneously, is born in the *Amor Veneris*, causing
this organ to send the *kinetic fluids* toward the brain, as a
harbinger of its desires. The brain then releases masses of new
fluids, to put in motion the mechanisms of seduction and to
nourish, at the same time, all the muscles that take part in
copulation. That is how desire for the male member is born.
But because the woman lacks a soul capable of mastering these
impulses, the sinful act will only be possible if she manages
successfully to entice a man with her seductive arts. It is as if
woman were the willpower of the flesh and man that of the
soul. According to whether one or the other gains the upper
hand, sinful behavior will or will not take place. Let us now
consider a second possibility: what occurs in the woman's
body when sinful behavior does not take place, when the willpower of man's soul is victorious? I have said that in man the
seminal spirits return to the soul, regulating and stabilizing
the *kinetic fluids* in the body. However: what happens to the
seminal fluids in the woman when, after having been
produced, they can neither be released nor transformed into
soulful passions?'

SIXTEENTH SECTION

Concerning the Accumulation of Kinetic Fluids *in Women*

'THE FIRST OCCURRENCE WE CAN OBSERVE IS AN enlargement of the *Amor Veneris*, because of the accumulation of fluids. In some cases I've observed that this small protuberance can grow to the size of a child's penis. At last, when these fluids can no longer be contained, they are released but internally, inside the body, causing all manner of ills, as is frequent in women. Many times, the sicknesses caused by the accumulation of *kinetic fluids* can be confused with demonic possession, and in fact, if the Devil were to choose a place in the body to make his lair, most certainly he would choose the *Amor Veneris*. The ancient Greeks believed that the uterus was the source of all kinds of diseases; I believe that all these diseases have their root in the organ it was my fate to discover. Now, if the process of sexual desire occurs in women naturally and spontaneously, as I've said, you must ask yourselves why there are women who are neither ugly nor gaunt with age, yet don't awaken man's desire or show lust for his member but, on the contrary, are kind and pious and can even bestow love like a man, that is to say, chaste love. There are several reasons for this.'

SEVENTEENTH SECTION

Concerning the Reason for Good Women Who Show No Inclination to Sin

'THE MOST COMMON REASON IS VIRGINITY. IF YOU HAVE never tasted venison, you will not lust after it. The *Amor Veneris* begins to exert its influence only after the hymen is ruptured. It is a common belief that the loss of virtue is a consequence of the appetites of the male member; I assure you that the latter is the fruit of the former.'

The dean interrupted.

'Permit me to point out that you are lost in a contradiction. If, as you say, woman is the object of sin, and man its subject, and if, still according to your words, the former naturally and spontaneously awakes sexual desire in the latter, what then leads a woman to lose her virtue, since no sexual appetite can arise in her because, according to you, this *Amor Veneris* of yours doesn't exercise its lustful influence while the maidenhead remains intact?'

'Your Excellency has anticipated the remarks I was about to make. Indeed, there appears to be no reason for a woman to relinquish her virtue since, while the hymen remains uncleft, the *Amor Veneris* has no active function. I could put forward in my favor the argument that a virgin, when offered in matrimony, becomes the victim of her husband's lust, inciting them to copulation. And yet, I anticipated Your Excellency's objection. I have said that sexual appetite awakens in men when their sensitive organs are excited by an external object of lust, that is to say, a woman whose venereal frenzy has been unleashed inside her body, for the temptation and seduction of men. I have also said that no-one can desire venison without having tasted it first. That which moves a virgin to lose her virtue is not the desire for the male member, but another equally natural and spontaneous desire: I mean the maternal instinct.

'The gestation of a child requires the massive release of *kinetic fluids*, both to sustain the excessive muscular activity during pregnancy, and to lend the new being its stable quantum of fluids. I have already repeated Aristotle's explanation of conception: man lends the child a soul, if the child is a boy, and woman a substance.

'There are open to women two paths of virtue: virginity or motherhood, and two paths of corruption: sin and sickness.

'When men steer away from sin by means of their free will, they also steer women away from sinful behavior: man it is who must lead woman down the path of virtue.'

EIGHTEENTH SECTION

Concerning the Reason Why the Amor Veneris *is Proof of the Genesis of Women in Keeping with the Holy Scriptures*

'ALLOW ME NOW TO POINT OUT TO YOU CERTAIN OTHER anatomical characteristics of the *Amor Veneris*. I have spoken to you of the shape of this organ, and of its functions, and of its influences on women's behavior. As this Excellent Committee will have been able to ascertain, not one of my words deviates in any way from the Scriptures; on the contrary, my words have no other purpose than to understand the magnificent Work of our Lord and, in this manner, give praise to the Creator. By this method it was granted me to reaffirm, in anatomical terms, another of the Sacred Truths of which the Scriptures speak. I refer to the genesis of woman. Human anatomy is like a book whose characters, if properly read, wonderfully reveal to us the Word. I say, most categorically, that the *Amor Veneris* is proof positive of the Word of God in verses twenty-two and twenty-three of the second chapter of the Book of Genesis. The organ of which I speak is the anatomical vestige of woman's begetter; the male shape of the *Amor Veneris* confirms that, as it is said in the Scriptures, the female is fashioned from the rib of the male.'

NINETEENTH SECTION

Concerning a Comparison Between the Male Member and *the* Amor Veneris

'I HAVE SEEN IN YOUR FACES THE HORROR, WHEN I TOLD you that the organ, of which I was granted the discovery, resembles a penis and that, like a penis, it rises and falls. And in truth, the *Amor Veneris* behaves apparently just like a penis, even though, quite obviously, they are not identical. The principal difference is physiological rather than anatomical, since the penis is but a means, an instrument, and the *Amor Veneris* a cause. Let me say that the male member, whether it is engorged or flaccid, depends on the avatars of body and soul, as I have already explained, while on the *Amor Veneris* depends all female behavior. Another anatomist, the great Leonardo da Vinci, has said that the male member has a life of its own, that it is an animal with its own soul and intelligence, independent from that of its master and acting according to its own will. And he said that, even though a man may wish to arouse it, it might disobey, moving of its own accord, without permission or desire on the part of its master, whether he be awake or asleep, doing as it pleases. And in truth, this seems confirmed in many cases. However, I will say that it is so only in appearance. When the male member rises inopportunely, without an apparent reason, that is to say, without the intervention of an external and lascivious object, there is a different explanation from that offered by Leonardo. The reason for the penis's becoming engorged without an apparent cause is simply that the *kinetic fluids*, produced for a specific function, have been diverted from their true path. For instance, that function may have been postponed or suspended, as happens when we prepare for a particular task and an unforeseen event prevents us from accomplishing it. The body prepares the muscles for their intended duties, and provides those muscles with a certain amount of *kinetic fluids*. According to the mechanics I've described, if the body is prevented from carrying out this task, it must find the means to rid itself of these fluids. It isn't difficult to join these two facts into a relationship of cause and effect; you can easily ascertain that when the penis becomes engorged of its own account, this invariably takes place immediately after we have postponed a task for which we were preparing ourselves. It is easy enough to rid ourselves of these fluids since they have not yet produced semen in the male member and, just as they have deviated from their natural course into the penis, they can take another channel from there toward other muscles. There they can be released through evaporation, by performing a task that will demand an equivalent volume of fluids. For similar reasons, sometimes, when a man has decided to commit a sin of the flesh, and even after he has paid in advance for his ill purpose, his member will on occasion fail to collaborate. This is because at times we remain ignorant of the designs that our own soul imposes on our body, when our soul separates itself from our will and forces our body to side with it.[18]

'Now, everything the great Leonardo said about the male member can be applied, with even stronger arguments, to the *Amor Veneris* which not only possesses a life, a will and an intelligence of its own, but a life, a will and an intelligence that guide the behavior of the being within which it is contained.[19] This is how we must understand female will and intelligence: as the will and intelligence of the *Amor Veneris*.

'Men must behave with women in the same way as the soul behaves with the body, since man's body is female just as his soul is male.

'I will end my plea in the certainty that everything I have said is just and true, and in perfect accordance with the Holy Scriptures. Let Justice be done.'

[18] Note that here Mateo Colombo demolishes his dualist argument (body/soul, female/male, sin/virtue) and introduces a third element that dissociates the will from both body and soul. He gives no evidence to support this enigmatic affirmation.

[19] This is the definition of woman that stems from Mateo Colombo's theory: the flesh surrounding the *Amor Veneris*.

THE SENTENCE

THE MIRACLE

I

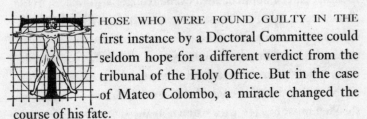HOSE WHO WERE FOUND GUILTY IN THE first instance by a Doctoral Committee could seldom hope for a different verdict from the tribunal of the Holy Office. But in the case of Mateo Colombo, a miracle changed the course of his fate.

The very day on which the committee was to give its verdict, a messenger from Rome arrived in Padua with a letter for the committee's president. Cardinal Caraffa read and reread the letter, and couldn't help feeling that the ground had been removed from under his feet. The letter carried the seal of Pope Paul III. The health of the septuagenarian pontiff was rapidly failing and the Holy Father himself personally requested the services of Mateo Colombo. The anatomist's reputation in Rome was certainly not that of a man destined for sainthood, rather the contrary. But it was also true that, largely thanks to his detractors, Mateo Colombo had become the best-known doctor in Europe. Even though his closest advisers tried to persuade His Holiness of the inappropriateness of the choice, Alessandro Farnese, with the bare whiff of life left in his body, was sufficiently stubborn to wish to decide for himself on matters regarding his own health. And he was still sufficiently feared to be able to impose his holy will. In such circumstances, the committee presided over by Cardinal Caraffa was forced to produce an urgent verdict in favor of the accused, though not in favor of his work. Mateo Colombo was declared innocent, and the doctors decided not to bring the case before the tribunal of the Holy Office. They did agree, however, to maintain the ban imposed by the dean on *De re anatomica*. A Solomon-like decision which, far from satisfying those concerned, disappointed and surprised everyone, including the bishops themselves.

The doctors' intent, according to precedent as well as their natural predisposition, favored the luminous path to the stake already proposed by the dean. Given the dean's influence on the doctors, the committee had condemned the anatomist even before he had uttered a single word in his defense, and had readied itself for the harshest of all sentences. Not because it considered the anatomist's investigations to be the work of the Devil; on the contrary, Mateo Colombo's discovery was a wonderful revelation to the doctors. The *Amor Veneris* finally explained one of the greatest enigmas and most obscure conundrums for the Church: the mystery of woman. But the problem was not only the discovery but also the discoverer. And without doubt, if this matter were widely known, the effects would be disastrous. If things were as the anatomist proposed, then the *Amor Veneris* would become a true instrument of power over the volatile female will. The publicizing of such a discovery would lead, most certainly, to all manner of misfortune. What would happen if Mateo Colombo's findings fell into the hands of the enemies of the Church? What calamities would Christendom have to face if the female object of sin fell into the hands of the Devil's hordes or, worse still, if the daughters of Eve themselves realized that between their legs they carried the keys to Heaven and Hell? The logic behind the discovery was this: if the *Amor Veneris* was the organ governing female will, the art of medicine would become that which granted control over its lascivious power. Consequently, whosoever had control over this organ would necessarily have control over the will of women. And how did one gain control over this *Amor Veneris*? By means of the learned art of medicine or even surgery. Knowing how to touch. Knowing how to slice.

Without doubt, the best fate for *De re anatomica* was for it to become the Church's jealously guarded secret and enter one of the catalogs of forbidden books, the *Indices librorum prohibitorum*. But who could guarantee Mateo Colombo's silence, even under oath? How to be certain that the anatomist himself might not try to profit from his discovery of the *Amor Veneris*? On the other hand, the discovery might allow the Church itself to find a Holy Remedy to guide its delicate and unwieldy flock down the path of virtue and saintliness; for instance, by removing the Devil's lair from inside the female body. If this organ was responsible for sinful behavior, then why not free women, at the very moment of birth, from this lascivious *Amor Veneris*? Did the Jews not cut off the prepuce of their male children? They certainly had their reasons. But these were still mere speculations. The all-important and immediate question was how to drown in silence, by whatever means possible, the dangerous matter. The committee began to draw up a sentence that left the way clear for the tribunal of the Holy Office.

The writings, however, were not destined for the same fate as their author. *De re anatomica* entered the murky catalogs of the censor, the *Indices librorum prohibitorum* that Pope Paul III himself had started in 1543. Under oath, the anatomist swore not to divulge his discovery. Under this condition, he was allowed to remain alive.

On the same day on which Cardinal Caraffa received the letter from Rome, on 7 November 1558, the Committee of Doctors gave its verdict, clearly intended for the eyes of one specific reader only.

THE VERDICT

I

VERDICT OF THE COMMITTEE OF DOCTORS, ADDRESSED TO THE DEAN OF THE UNIVERSITY OF PADUA

'WE, THE UNDERSIGNED, HAVE TAKEN INTO CONSIDERATION the depositions, documents and pleas presented to this committee by you requested, regarding the Present Occupant of the Chair of Anatomy, author of *De re anatomica*, the *chirologo* Mateo Renaldo Colombo, at the University of Padua over which you preside.

'This committee fails to understand the hostility you have shown toward your Chair and the contradictions which you incur in your choleric considerations, if consideration and wrath can be companions in thought. This may be the reason for the blindness that prevents you from seeing matters as they really are.

'Honorable Dean: regarding your dissatisfaction with and hostile criticism of *De re anatomica*, in particular of Chapter XVII, we can only judge by your version since, as you say yourself, "the work is held in my most jealous care".

'Our understanding, however, cannot follow your reasoning. First you brand your anatomist's discovery as an absurdity; then you accuse him of plagiarism and theft, arguing that the organ in question has already been described in Antiquity by Rufus of Ephesus, Julius Polux, the Arab anatomists Abulcassis and Avicenna, Hippocrates and even Gabriele Fallopio. You must decide: either we assume the former premise and affirm that no such organ exists, or we embrace the latter, and declare that the organ is as well known to science as Adam's apple.

'We, for our part, have no knowledge of any previous description of such an organ. We are unable to affirm its existence or its inexistence.

'Even if its existence were confirmed, we believe that your obviously venerable efforts to defend the Sacred Principles, and your fear that such a discovery might incite to heresy and augment the number of unbelievers, are honorable in spite of being mistaken. Truth lies in the Scriptures and nowhere else. Science does not reveal it: science is barely a feeble flame lighting the Handwriting of God. Science is below God and serves to make the Truth comprehensible. We of the faith know that faith is enough, but the unbelievers cannot be persuaded of the Truth unless Reason convinces them.

'What you fail to see, Honorable Dean, is that if the discovery of your anatomist were proven to be true, we would have before our very eyes, at long last, the anatomical proof of the creation of Woman as told in the Holy Scriptures. If you refer to the appropriate verses in the Book of Genesis, you will find confirmation of what we say.

'In conclusion, and following our arguments above, we declare the accused, Mateo Renaldo Colombo, to be innocent of all charges. Nevertheless, this tribunal disallows the publication of *De re anatomica*, and consigns it to the *Indices librorum prohibitorum*.'

PART FOUR

THE HOLY ARTS

I

N 8 NOVEMBER 1558, UNDER THE INDIGNANT nose of Alessandro di Legnano, Mateo Colombo left for Rome flanked by a Vatican escort. The Pope's personal physician was traveling in princely fashion and everyone addressed him with the deference due to an Eminent Person. However, both the dean and the anatomist knew that his luck was as vulnerable as the Pope's fragile health.

Alessandro Farnese was lying in his Vatican bed. The over-grown and disheveled beard gave him the look of a decrepit rabbi. Mateo Colombo knelt to one side of the bed, took the pontifical hand and, kissing the ring, found it hard to hold back the tears when the Pope, with failing strength, blessed him in a barely audible whisper. Composing himself, the anatomist demanded that he be left alone with His Holiness, a demand that of course was not obeyed. Alessandro Farnese was barely more than skin hanging over bones. He had been an old man when he was elected Pope, at the age of sixty-six, and he had survived almost every illness known to humanity. He was no longer the man who had managed to unite the Princes of the Church against the Turks; he was certainly no longer the man who had, first through patience and then through sheer force, succeeded in gathering the Council of Trent. He was no longer the man who had, with holy endurance, submitted to the whims of the Duke of Mantua, the Emperor and the Protestants. And he was no longer the man who had so ardently defended the tribunals of the Inquisition, whose bonfires he had deemed insufficient to purify the souls of such an immensity of sinners, and whose judges he thought too few and bureaucratic, consequently multiplying them as Christ had done with the loaves and fishes, conferring on them ambulatory faculties, elevating them to the rank of Superior Tribunals in matters of faith, and nominating delegates in Venice, Milan, Naples, Tuscany and wherever his fancy dictated. Nor was he any longer the voracious reader who would decide, in person, what books were to be consigned either to the *Indices librorum prohibitorum* or to the flames, together with their authors, of course. Alessandro Farnese was no longer that man but his own ghost, decrepit and dying. His scrawny hand, whose nepotic index finger had attempted to secularize the bishoprics of Parma and Piacenza in order to transform them into principalities under the rule of the Farnese, now rested, motionless, between the hands of the demonic anatomist from Cremona, who had been so timely rescued from Hell and conducted to Paradise. His Eminence was placing himself in the hands of the man who, until yesterday, was Lucifer's voice and, today, the hand of God.

The condition of Paul III was worrisome, not only for His Holiness but also for his new personal physician, whose life depended on the pontifical health. After examining him for several hours, Mateo Colombo came to the uneasy certainty that there was little that could be done; Alessandro Farnese had never been entirely cured of the illness that, five years earlier, had led him to the edge of the grave. In fact, the anatomist could hardly explain how the old man had survived so long. The Pope's heart beat without conviction, his skin had already acquired the color of the dead, and he spoke with a barely audible asthmatic voice: every phrase demanded an exhausting effort and his attempts to regain his old loquacity were systematically interrupted by fits of dry coughing that choked him and made his skin turn purple. When these fits ceased, the green hue that had been his for the past six months would return to his face. He barely cared now about the gout that had troubled him all his life or the epileptic fits, or the ancient migraines, or the horrible herpes that lashed his skin, causing him to grow his Semitic beard. Paul III was dying. His Holiness had himself dismissed the incompetent doctor appointed to him by that crook Cardinal Alvarez de Toledo, who, according to His Holiness, wished to succeed him as soon as possible. Whether that was true or not, it was certain that since this doctor had begun looking after his health, Alessandro Farnese had deteriorated visibly from day to day. Mateo Colombo agreed with his patient. The therapy recommended by his predecessor was more noxious than the illness itself; therefore the new pontifical physician ordered that the blood-letting should stop, since it only aggravated the Holy Father's anemia; that the enemas be suspended, since they left him exhausted; and he expressly forbade the administration of emetic herbs. The correct therapy did not consist of an attempt to purge the sickness through all the holy orifices. All the previous doctor had managed to do was to smother the few embers of life that still glowed in the ancient body of the Pope.

Mateo Colombo ordered that, for one entire day, the pontifical stools should be collected in a jar and, in another, the holy urinary fluids. During the night, the anatomist examined the contents of both jars, scrupulously considering the scent, color and viscosity. And before the sun was up, Mateo Colombo had decided on the appropriate treatment. In fact, Paul III's only illness was that of his own advanced age.

The Holy Father had to live. Mateo Colombo would have been ready to give the decrepit Alessandro Farnese half of his own life. But there was another alternative.

Paul III needed young blood. That was exactly what the anatomist would give him.

THE FEAST OF THE HOLY
INNOCENTS

I

N THE FEAST OF THE HOLY INNOCENTS AND with the Holy Father's consent, Mateo Renaldo Colombo, newly appointed doctor to Pope Paul III, ordered that ten young girls be chosen, between the ages of five and ten, in obvious good health, and brought to the pontifical rooms. He personally selected five of the ten and brought them to the bedside of His Holiness. The ancient Pontiff blessed each of the five, who wept with emotion when kissing his ring, and who were then led to a room which had been made ready for them close to that of the anatomist. Having done this, Mateo Colombo ordered a search for the sturdiest wet-nurses in Rome. He then chose three of the best-looking ones, three young women with magnificent breasts and an admirable complexion. The anatomist thought it necessary to test the quality of their milk, and he personally sampled the taste and consistency of the fluid that issued generously when the nipples were lightly stimulated by his fingers.

Three times a day, His Holiness was fed with the nourishing

milk of the young women; like a child, he would curl up against the breast of one of the wet-nurses and drink until falling into a deep sleep. It was touching to see the old Alessandro Farnese, toothless and white-bearded, cradled in this manner. This therapy proved useful but insufficient, since the women's milk carried valuable *kinetic fluids* but too few to restore to the Pope his long-lost youth. Therefore, earlier than he had foreseen, Mateo Colombo summoned to his rooms the most skillful executioner in Rome.

The executioner felt offended when the anatomist asked him to be as gentle as possible. After all, this was his profession.

That very evening, before the Feast of the Holy Innocents came to a close, the first of the five young girls was executed.

His Holiness, before drinking the first drop of the bloody infusion, said a prayer for the child's soul which no doubt had preceded his to the Kingdom of Heaven, and he rejoiced in her happy and early fate.

'Amen,' he said and he emptied his cup to the lees.

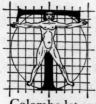HREE TIMES A DAY PAUL III WAS NURSED ON
breast-milk and, three times a day, he drank
down to the last drop the infusions of young
blood that his doctor, Mateo Renaldo
Colombo, personally prepared for him. Mateo
Colombo let out a sigh of relief when, after a week, he was able
to confirm that the Pope's health was improving. The treatment, except in its details, was far from original; Pope
Innocent VIII, the Pontiff who had made himself popular by
confessing publicly to his virility and recognizing his offspring
– Franceschetto, Battistina and Teodorina – had undergone,
under the recommendation of his doctor, a similar therapy in
his old age, except that on that occasion it had produced
unhappy results. According to the anatomist, the reasons for
that failure were not difficult to establish: first of all, the
nurses' milk was first drawn by servants and then served to the
Pontiff in glasses, and Mateo Colombo knew that the *kinetic
fluids* evaporated at once when in contact with the air. The milk
had to be drunk straight from the breast, just as the Almighty

had decreed. Secondly, the blood with which the infusion was prepared was extracted from young boys, when it was evident that female blood was pure substance, pure matter, as the great Aristotle had noted in his writings on gestation. Male blood was useless for this treatment since, as was well known, it consisted of pure spirits and little substance, like wine.

Whatever the reason, the health of Paul III seemed to improve.

The news reached Padua. Alessandro di Legnano oozed poison.

The Pope felt a personal liking for his physician. He had, of course, many reasons to like him. Among various small improvements, his old loquacity had returned and, between each breastfeed, the Holy Father conversed endlessly with Mateo Colombo, taking him into his confidence. Not surprisingly, the anatomist's old inquisitor, Cardinal Caraffa, felt that the intruder from Padua was like a thorn in the throat.

HEAVEN WITH BOTH HANDS

I

ATEO COLOMBO FELT HE WAS TOUCHING Heaven with both hands. During his time in Rome, the anatomist produced his greatest pictorial work: the most beautiful anatomical charts ever made, painted in exquisite oils, and hundreds of ink sketches of his obsession, the *Amor Veneris*. And it was during his Roman sojourn that he painted his strangest and most sublime creation: his *Hermes and Aphrodite*, a title that can be attributed only to the rigors of the censor, since the painting does not show the union of the two deities in a single body, but invokes instead the anatomist's vision of Inés de Torremolinos as she looked when he discovered his *Amor Veneris*.

Everything was an inspiration. Nothing was out of his reach. The stormy inquisitorial days were over. Now he could look at his former inquisitors from the right hand of Paul III's high throne, since he had restored the old man to life as Christ had done for Lazarus. The obscure anatomist from Cremona was now the instrument of God. His name was destined for glory.

He now lived in the City of Heaven on Earth. He had replaced his old linen *lucco* with a new one made of silk, and his cotton *beretta* with a gold-embroidered fez which the Pope's own tailor had made for him. He was a rich man. His fees as the Pontiff's personal physician were as high as he considered fair and, whenever he so wished, he was given access to the holy coffers. After all, how much was the life of His Holiness worth? Nothing touched him, no-one could measure up to him. He walked about the Vatican as if it all belonged to him. He was the only person allowed to enter the papal chambers without asking leave and whenever he wished. He was the only man permitted to interrupt pontifical meetings. He alone was allowed to give commands to the Holy Father, telling His Holiness when to eat, when to go to bed, when to be woken. He alone decided if it was convenient for His Holiness to receive a certain guest, and he alone watched over the fits of pontifical anger and the moments of pontifical calm.

But his happiness was not yet complete. Every night, before falling asleep, he would think of Mona Sofia. However, his anxiety at the prospect of their meeting was tempered by his conviction that she would belong to him. He was certain of this. No matter how many men desired her, not even how many enjoyed her body. The day would come when, free, rich and famous, he would climb the seven steps up to the Bordello del Fauno Rosso and then, like a general at whose feet an old enemy surrenders, he would take possession of his longed-for colony. He knew he had to be cautious and, above all, patient. From now on, he had to behave like a shrewd politician.

In the Vatican, no-one was unaware of the influence Mateo Colombo had over Paul III; this, his former tormentor,

Cardinal Alvarez de Toledo, knew full well. Seeing that he himself no longer had any influence over His Holiness, Alvarez de Toledo decided to befriend the Pope's personal physician. He knew what words would please the anatomist's ear. He knew how to flatter him.

Cardinal Caraffa, on the other hand, was unable to hide the visceral antipathy and scorn he felt for Mateo Colombo. Nor was he able to hide his resentment at the fact that the torch that was to light the bonfire had been snuffed out under his very nose.

As proof of trust and definitive reconciliation, Cardinal Alvarez de Toledo put his own health in the hands of the Pontiff's doctor. Mateo Colombo was fully aware that Alvarez de Toledo was the cardinal best placed to succeed Paul III; the Spaniard was indeed a crafty businessman.

II

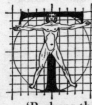RUSTING HIS LUCK, MATEO COLOMBO decided to inform His Holiness of the fate that had befallen his *De re anatomica*, hopeful that the ban imposed on it by Cardinal Caraffa might be lifted at last.

'Perhaps this is not the right moment,' was Paul III's only answer.

This was Mateo Colombo's first great disappointment. But he was patient and willing to wait.

'We shall see, later on we shall see . . .' was all the answer the anatomist got from the Pope when, six months later, he brought up the matter again.

Then Alessandro Farnese continued in a paternal tone: 'My son, you should seek confession because you have sinned greatly. You have told me about that which you swore to the committee not to reveal to anyone.'

Mateo Colombo felt both indignant and astonished. He had saved the Pope's life, and this was his thanks? Not only did His Holiness quench all hope of seeing *De re anatomica* published, but he even had the temerity to admonish his savior.

Mateo Colombo began to wish that the decrepit and thankless Alessandro Farnese would yield up his soul at last. After all, the anatomist was the instrument of God and, just as he was able to give life, as he had done for his dying patient, he could also take life away. Was he not the personal physician of the future Pontiff?

His friendship with Cardinal Alvarez de Toledo strengthened day by day; they shared a common desire and, every time they spoke of the health of His Holiness, they could not avoid sharing a common guilty look. They never breathed a word about their secret; there was obviously no need.

III

NE RAINY MORNING, PAUL III WAS FOUND dead. It was Mateo Colombo himself who brought the sad news. On that very same day, the conclave of cardinals was assembled. The outcome was not expected to be a surprise. Mateo Colombo felt he was on the verge of seeing his work finally published, and readied himself to kiss the ring of the new Pope, his friend, Cardinal Alvarez de Toledo. Calmly, since there was no reason for fear or uncertainty, the anatomist took his lunch in his rooms, after which he asked to be woken in mid-afternoon, and he lay down to sleep.

It was mid-afternoon when he leaned out of the window of his bedroom and looked toward the basilica. No smoke was yet visible. He decided to stay in his quarters because he didn't want to hear whatever rumors might be spreading through the palace. Night was falling when he looked through the window again. He felt somewhat uneasy at the lack of a sign in the darkling sky. Why was the news taking so long, if the choice had already been made?

But then he felt calm again.

It was pitch dark when the anatomist decided to sit by the window until the white smoke could be seen.

THE LAST SUPPER

I

T MIDNIGHT PRECISELY, THE BASILICA'S chimney released a very thin column of white smoke. All the Vatican bells resounded and all the archways began to spew forth crowds running toward St Peter's Square. A flock of frightened pigeons flew around the basilica's dome. Everything suddenly lit up. The anatomist's heart filled with a long-contained anxiety. From his window he could see the Pope's balcony perfectly. He laughed out loud as he hadn't laughed in years. The gathered crowd was shouting out for the new Pope. Like seeds in the wind, the name of the new Pontiff flew from mouth to mouth. He would be called Paul IV. But which of the cardinals would be Paul IV? 'Alvarez de Toledo' was the name that could be read on the lips of the people.

Preceded by a deathly silence, in an atmosphere of tension, emotion and respect, His Holiness finally appeared on the balcony. Mateo Colombo was still laughing as he had never laughed before. Only when the anatomist's exultation subsided and he was able to open wide his eyes, could he see clearly the face of Paul IV. His heart turned inside him. His laughter froze. The man raising his arms on the balcony was none other than Cardinal Caraffa.

He thought he could see, across the distance, the new Pope bestowing a glance in his direction.

I I

HAT VERY NIGHT, MATEO COLOMBO packed his things. There was no reason to wait; not only would his work be definitively banned, but he was certain that his former inquisitor would execute the sentence that had previously been suspended. He knew the depth of Caraffa's hatred for him.

And yet, all was not lost. He considered his options and reached an immediate decision. He still had his much-desired sanctuary in Venice. He had not forgotten his reason for living. And nothing in the world could now prevent Mona Sofia from, at long last, giving him her heart. After all, the anatomist had in his hands the key to the will of any woman he chose. And the woman he chose was his Mona Sofia.

Furthermore, he was now a wealthy man, possessed of a fortune that he would be unable to spend in one lifetime. And it would not be difficult to escape Caraffa's guards. In a couple of minutes he decided the course of the rest of his existence: he would leave for Venice, go to the Bordello del Fauno Rosso, pay the ten ducats that would allow him to buy Mona Sofia's love, and from Venice they would leave for the far coast of the Mediterranean or, if necessary, for the new lands at the other end of the world, beyond the Atlantic Ocean.

Then, madly in love with the anatomist, Mona Sofia would become the most loyal of women and the most faithful of wives.

So that very night he packed some clothes and all the money he had earned during his stay in the Vatican. He pulled his *foggia* over his forehead and, walking against the crowd, he lost himself like a criminal in the crooked alleys of Rome.

Behind him, the Vatican was joyfully celebrating.

PART FIVE

THE BLACK MASS

I

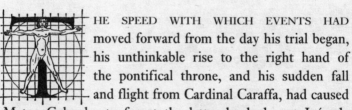HE SPEED WITH WHICH EVENTS HAD moved forward from the day his trial began, his unthinkable rise to the right hand of the pontifical throne, and his sudden fall and flight from Cardinal Caraffa, had caused Mateo Colombo to forget the letter he had sent Inés de Torremolinos from his cell at the university. It might be said that he had forgotten entirely about the existence of his former patron. He thought of Mona Sofia as his unavoidable destiny; the day would come (as it did, sooner than he had expected) on which he would have to leave the Vatican: he would then travel to Venice and, in the bordello of Via Bocciari, he would meet his predestined prize. He didn't think about that long-awaited moment with anxiety, but with that fatalism which allows us to bear the certainty of our death. During his Vatican sojourn, however, he had not thought even once of the faraway Inés de Torremolinos.

The fact is that, as fate would have it, thanks to the good offices of Messer Vittorio, the letter had indeed reached Florence.

II

NE APRIL DAWN IN THE YEAR 1558, A messenger called at the door of the unassuming house close to the abbey. From the day Mateo Colombo had left Florence, Inés had not had news from the anatomist. Yet from that very same day, she had thought of nothing but Mateo Colombo and everything in the world reminded her of him. So many times, upon the arrival of a messenger, she had felt with mistaken confidence that there would be news from him, that to avoid further disillusionment she had become determined never again to contemplate the possibility, and she now refused even to look at the wax seal that held the ribbon around the scroll. She walked with it to the small scriptorium where her daughters were singing and playing. Only once she was seated at the desk did she allow herself to look at the seal. Her heart missed a beat. Trying to remain calm or, at least, to appear it, she quietly ordered the girls to continue their games in their bedroom. Before undoing the ribbon, she pressed the letter to her breast and said a prayer. So many months she had

been waiting for this moment. And yet now, after all her endless anguish and disappointment, now that at last she was able to touch at least the very paper that the anatomist's hands had touched, a great sadness overcame her. Something told her that the letter brought no good tidings. She drew it out of its binding.

She had to hold onto the edge of the desk so as not to fall off her chair when she read: 'When this letter reaches you in Florence, I will no longer be alive . . .' Her eyes full of tears and her body convulsed, she continued to read: 'Should you consider that I am committing a sacrilege by speaking out when I have sworn to keep silent, stop reading now and throw these papers into the flames . . .' And even though she did believe that the anatomist was committing a sacrilege, she carried on reading.

If I have decided to break the vows of silence imposed upon me and if I have resolved to reveal to you alone my discovery, it is because it was in your body, my lady, that I found my sweet 'America'. In your body I found the seat of love and of supreme pleasure in women. And you I must thank for revealing God's Work as regards female love. My Amor Veneris *is your* Amor Veneris. *Do not think I don't know how much you have loved me. And even today perhaps it is so. But do not be deceived; it is not me that you love. Nor is it you who loves me. When I cured you of your sickness, unwittingly I replaced it with that love that you profess toward me. Your sickness resided in the* Amor Veneris *and it is your* Amor Veneris *which is now in love with me. Do not be deceived. I am no one, my lady, to deserve your love.*

Inés de Torremolinos finished reading the letter impassively. Her eyes were still damp but her heart now beat with sudden calm. Suddenly her eyes filled with quiet determination. She stood up and walked into the kitchen. She took up a knife and a whetstone. She considered the situation serenely. She lamented greatly the supposed death of her beloved, expressed deep condolences and was even grateful for them. While sharpening the knife on the stone, she felt reason clearing her mind like a new light. Many times she had been haunted by dark fears of madness and death. But now, whetting the blade on the stone, she told herself that this was her moment of highest and most sublime lucidity. Her hand was not guided by a mystical impulse or an ecstatic rapture. She had never felt more at peace.

'*Amor Veneris vel Dulcedo Apeletur,*' she chanted, while sharpening the knife.

She continued sharpening the blade with the same calm with which she rang the abbey bells every morning. Now, at last, she would be the mistress of her own heart. She did not even feel anguish at the thought that the anatomist had known all along that she was madly in love with him. So many hours of suffering could have been avoided, had she but known! It was all so easy now.

After making certain that the blade was perfectly sharp, she lifted her eyes and looked out of the windows, filling her soul with the landscape. The cut was quick and precise. She felt no pain and there was hardly any bleeding; barely a thin thread of blood rolled down her thigh. Between her index finger and her thumb, she now held the cause of all her torments. She looked at the tiny organ and said with a beatific smile:

'*Amor Veneris vel Dulcedo Apeletur.*'

From now on and for ever, she would do without love. At last, she was the mistress of her own heart.

THE RESURRECTION OF THE FLESH

I

ROM THAT DAY ONWARDS, NOTHING more was heard in Florence of Inés de Torremolinos. From that April morning on which a messenger had knocked on the door of the small house next to the abbey, the abbot had no more news of his benefactress and her three daughters. All the abbot found on the kitchen floor were a few thin threads of blood and, next to a knife and a whetstone, four minuscule and identical pieces of flesh, four red pearls whose anatomical provenance the abbot was unable to identify. Inés de Torremolinos and her three daughters had vanished from Florence.

Inés had been a step away from sainthood, but even one step can separate the snows of virtue from the flames at the stake. Because Inés de Torremolinos (now it must be said), after a brief trial in the Castile of her birth, ended her days on the bonfire of the Holy Office in the year 1559. She uttered not a word in her own defense.

The proof that determined her fate was a book of verses

whose authorship she admitted. It was no doubt a minor sin, compared to the others of which she stood accused and to which she pleaded guilty. *The Black Mass* (this was the title under which the book was known) was burnt next to its author and, as with her biography, of which nothing but some random details survive, only a few verses were saved in the oral tradition. Of the sixty poems that made up *The Black Mass*, fragments of just seven are known today.[20]

---

[20] The complete original Spanish version was never found and, presumably, all copies were burnt. The seven surviving poems have been translated from the Italian, collected in the *Antologia Proibita*.

THE BLACK MASS

I

Poems

1

If leaping flames are lit for me,
Or hemlock down my gullet pours
Or if I'm hanged from Judas' tree
Yes, even then my joy endures,
For I declare myself to be
The world's most whorish Whore of Whores.

14

All we do we do for love.
Gratify the gallows' cove,
Busy baking for his sake,
In exchange a crumb we take.
Making babes to toil and rove,
All we do we do for love.
Since a loaf he cannot bake,
Since a child he cannot make,
Artless in the craft of bread,
Useless in the birthing-bed,
Let him bake his bread of grass,
Let him foal out of his ass.

22

Love was for me
sickness and ache,
dagger and stake . . .

. . . . . .

If singing of love
I only knew sorrow
And lovesick tomorrow . . .

. . . . . .

43

Condemned to the kitchen,
My recipe read,
Its long-guarded secret
Will answer your need.

Go find twenty shepherds
And breakfast there quick
By choosing the sturdiest
And milking his prick,
A thirst-quenching nectar
The best you can pick.

At Mass you must never
Communion wine lick;
The host is too meager,
The meal is too quick.
Commune with the father
And lunch on his prick.

II

HE FIRST POEM IS THE SUMMING–UP OF THE tragedy. It consists of a declaration of princi- ples and also, perhaps, a foretelling of her fate. Inés de Torremolinos was not only 'the world's most whorish Whore of Whores', not only the most expensive and sought-after whore in Spain. During the long year of 1559, which seemed to her longer than her entire life, she founded the most perfect caste of whores in all of the Mediterranean. There was no need to bring them up as if they were royalty, no need to educate their spirit to reject affection, nor to train their body in abstinence from pleasure, since they would never suffer from love-pangs or become slaves to pleasure. During the long year of 1559, Inés de Torremolinos not only exercised and taught the art of prosti- tution with masterly craft. She became a fervent missionary in the cause of freeing female hearts from bondage. During that very long year, Inés de Torremolinos made, with her body, a fortune several times greater than that which she had inherited from her father and her husband. She built the most splendid

brothels and recruited her pupils among the most tortured souls. From irredeemably besotted young girls to cloistered nuns, all listened to the inflammatory sermons of Inés de Torremolinos. Each of them had in her hands the means to be, at long last, mistress of her own heart.

More than fifteen hundred women worked in the brothels of Inés de Torremolinos. More than fifteen hundred women had chosen the road of freedom and forsworn the curse of the *Amor Veneris*. In every case, the ablation was done by Inés de Torremolinos herself. Not a single man shared in the enormous wealth garnered by the business. It was a true army of female willpower.

III

HE *BLACK MASS* VERSES BECAME A FEARFUL catechism. There was not a single woman who, on hearing them, did not feel she could identify with at least one of its lines: women married and unmarried, widows and nuns, lovesick girls and jilted spinsters. *The Black Mass* was a title that referred to all women, since it hinted at covens and the dark initiation rites of witches. And witches were clearly described by the authorities. In the so-called *Catalog of Witches and Harpies*, this precise definition could be found:

She who causes another ill; she who shows evil intent; she who casts sidelong looks; she who stares into the eyes unabashed; she who goes out at night; she who nods off during the day; she who is sad; she who laughs excessively; she who is distracted; she who is devout; she who is easily frightened; she who is courageous and stern; she who goes to confession often; she who never goes to confession; she who defends herself; she who accuses by pointing with the index finger; she who has

knowledge of distant events; she who knows the secrets of art and science; she who speaks many languages.

Prostitution was not a punishable offense. But witchcraft, of course, was. The *Catalog of Witches and Harpies* had a ready-made definition for each and every case.

PART SIX

THE TRINITY

I

ARLY ONE WINTER MORNING OF THE YEAR 1559, shortly before sunrise, a handful of people, perhaps seeking warmth because of the cruel Castilian weather, gathered in a tight circle in the market square, to watch the executioner light his faggots. In the middle, tied to the stake, was Inés de Torremolinos. Behind her stood three other stakes that towered above her three short daughters.

'Burn the witches!' the women shouted, putting their children on their shoulders so that they could watch the exemplary spectacle.

First the executioner lit the faggots on which the girls' feet were resting. Their cries, the judges had declared, would multiply the torment of the Mother Witch. However, when the branches were fully engulfed, none of the girls let out a single cry. Before their small bodies could become completely disfigured by the tongues of fire climbing to the top of the stakes, they were already dead, asphyxiated by the smoke.

It seemed as if what was being slowly roasted in the rising heat was the insensitive skin of a salamander, not the delicate skin of a woman. Inés de Torremolinos bore the flames with a beatific look and it seemed as if her slight body, were it not fastened to the stake, might rise in the black smoke billowing from the burnt flesh of her ankles. As if animated by the Almighty, she was able to resist without complaint a temperature a thousand times greater than that of her body.

Suddenly, in a gust of wind, a tongue of fire engulfed her completely; when the flame subsided, it left behind an unrecognizable body, black and shapeless. She was still alive. The executioner fanned the flames and saw in the eyes of the condemned woman a look of pity. For a moment, the executioner felt human, or at least something close to human, as a wave of shame swept over him; then the woman, or what was left of her, died.

The bells of the basilica had just struck the hour.

I I

T THAT SAME HOUR, BUT IN VENICE, A man with his face hidden under his *foggia* was walking quickly down Via Bocciari. He walked as if determined to reach his destination before the sun rose between the columns holding up the winged lion and St Theodore, before the automata in the clock tower struck the first chime of six o'clock. Before climbing the steps of the Bordello del Fauno Rosso, the man adjusted his *foggia* and made sure he was not seen by any of the passersby on their way to early Mass at the Church of the Holy Trinity.

Madonna Simoneta greeted him and immediately invited him in.

'Are you familiar with the service at this house?' she asked and, seeing that the visitor made no answer, she offered him a catalog and a glass of wine, believing him to be a timid traveler.

It seemed as if the man wished to remain anonymous, since he retained the hood that covered his face. He had taken no notice of the glass he had been offered.

'I want to see Mona Sofia,' the man said laconically.

The woman said nothing and lowered her eyes.

'I know it is early,' he excused himself, 'but it is urgent.'

'Who wants to see her?' muttered the woman without raising her eyes.

Mateo Colombo couldn't understand the reason for all this formality.

'I'm an old client,' was all he said.

'I'm afraid she can't see you.'

'I can wait if she's busy, but I don't have much time.'

The anatomist noticed that the woman's eyes filled with tears. He grabbed her by the arms and shook her violently.

'What is the matter?' he shouted and ran toward the stairs leading to the upper floor.

'For God's sake, I beg you, don't enter her room!' the woman cried, trying to hold him back by his *lucco*.

III

HE SIGHT THAT GREETED MATEO COLOMBO when he entered Mona Sofia's room made his blood turn cold. He felt terrified, and overwhelmed. It was, quite precisely, the end of his world.

The stench in the room made it difficult to breathe. In the middle of the bed lay a suffering and mutilated thing, a skeleton covered in a few rotting shreds of skin, greyish green, dotted with purple tumors. Mateo Colombo approached, holding himself steady against the wall. He was only able to recognize that these living remains were Mona Sofia's by the eyes, green as emeralds, jutting from her face with a lunatic expression.

Never, in all his life as a doctor, had he ever witnessed a case of syphilis so advanced. He pulled back the covers and saw the most macabre spectacle he had ever beheld. The firm animal thighs, as if carved in wood, were now two useless bones. The hands, so small that it seemed impossible for them to grasp an engorged member, were like two autumn twigs. The nipples, each as round and soft as a flower, if such a flower were possible . . .

Mateo Colombo sat by the side of the bed, caressed her hair – now thin and brittle – and her furrowed forehead. He was weeping. Not out of sorrow. Not out of compassion. He was weeping as lovers do. He loved every inch of that body decimated by disease. Delicately, he took hold of her ankles and, slowly, he parted her thighs. He saw the dry and faded vulva that seemed like the mouth of a toothless crone, pushed aside the folds of flesh and stroked her *Amor Veneris*. He caressed it softly, lovingly. He touched it with infinite tenderness. He wept with the emotion of love as it gripped him by the throat.

'My love,' he said to her from the depths of his soul, 'my love,' he repeated while all the time caressing his sweet 'America'.

The anatomist felt a gentle tremor in the flesh between his fingers and heard a whisper. His cheeks bathed in tears, he asked her:

'Do you love me?' It was a supplication, an entreaty.

Mona Sofia moved her eyes toward the window, took in as much breath as her ailing lungs would allow her, barely a mouthful of air, and without moving her lips, with a voice that seemed to come from the bottom of a cavern, she spoke:

'Your time is up,' he heard her say, before letting out a hoarse whisper, her last.

THE APEX

I

N THE HIGHEST PEAK OF THE MASSIVE promontory that separates Verona from Trento, on the top of Monte Veldo, a crow settles on a carcass still fresh. Before sinking his beak into the abundant dead flesh, he inhales the scent he likes best. It seems to be a long-awaited meal. He digs into one eye and shakes it until he is able to pluck it from its socket. He pulls it aside and then devours it. Then he walks along the carcass and sinks his beak into the wound from which emerges, like a shaft, the hilt of a knife. He eats until he is full. Before lifting off and flying toward Venice, before flying toward the Grand Canal where, any moment now, as every morning, the barge that collects the dead is about to pass, he perches on a bloated finger and pecks at it until the flesh comes loose. For the first time, Leonardino has eaten without fear out of his master's hand.

Tomorrow he will return for the rest.

A SELECTED LIST OF FINE WRITING
AVAILABLE FROM BLACK SWAN

99588	6	**THE HOUSE OF SPIRITS**	*Isabel Allende*	£7.99
99820	6	**FLANDERS**	*Patricia Anthony*	£6.99
99619	X	**HUMAN CROQUET**	*Kate Atkinson*	£6.99
99824	9	**THE DANDELION CLOCK**	*Guy Burt*	£6.99
99686	6	**BEACH MUSIC**	*Pat Conroy*	£7.99
99767	6	**SISTER OF MY HEART**	*Chitra Banerjee Divakaruni*	£6.99
99587	8	**LIKE WATER FOR CHOCOLATE**	*Laura Esquivel*	£6.99
99721	8	**BEFORE WOMEN HAD WINGS**	*Connie May Fowler*	£6.99
99848	6	**CHOCOLAT**	*Joanne Harris*	£6.99
99796	X	**A WIDOW FOR ONE YEAR**	*John Irving*	£7.99
99758	7	**FRIEDA AND MIN**	*Pamela Jooste*	£6.99
99037	X	**BEING THERE**	*Jerzy Kosinski*	£5.99
99807	9	**MONTENEGRO**	*Starling Lawrence*	£6.99
99580	0	**CAIRO TRILOGY I:**		
		PALACE WALK	*Naguib Mahfouz*	£7.99
99874	5	**PAPER**	*John McCabe*	£6.99
99762	5	**THE LACK BROTHERS**	*Malcolm McKay*	£6.99
99785	4	**GOODNIGHT, NEBRASKA**	*Tom McNeal*	£6.99
99718	8	**IN A LAND OF PLENTY**	*Tim Pears*	£6.99
99817	6	**INK**	*John Preston*	£6.99
99783	8	**DAY OF ATONEMENT**	*Jay Rayner*	£6.99
99810	9	**THE JUKEBOX QUEEN OF MALTA**	*Nicholas Rinaldi*	£6.99
99777	3	**THE SPARROW**	*Mary Doria Russell*	£6.99
99846	X	**THE WAR ZONE**	*Alexander Stuart*	£6.99
99819	2	**WHISTLING FOR THE ELEPHANTS**	*Sandi Toksvig*	£6.99
99780	3	**KNOWLEDGE OF ANGELS**	*Jill Paton Walsh*	£6.99
99673	4	**DINA'S BOOK**	*Herbjørg Wassmo*	£6.99